History of Hate

Kanishka Gupta is a literary consultant and freelance researcher. He has headed a men's lifestyle portal and edited the creative lifestyle magazine, Platform. He runs a Delhi-based literary agency.

History of Hate

Kanishka Gupta

RUPA

Published by
Rupa Publications India Pvt. Ltd 2010
7/16, Ansari Road, Daryaganj
New Delhi 110002

Sales centres:
Bengaluru Chennai
Hyderabad Jaipur Kathmandu
Kolkata Mumbai Prayagraj

This is a work of fiction. Names, characters, places and incidents are either the product of the author's imagination or are used fictitiously and any resemblance to any actual person, living or dead, events or locales is entirely coincidental.

P-ISBN: 978-81-291-1658-1
E-ISBN: 978-81-291-2644-3

Second impression 2023

10 9 8 7 6 5 4 3 2

Printed in India

To
my mother, Arti Gupta,
who always taught me
to be brave and forthright.

Contents

Acknowledgements

To Rahul Soni, beloved friend and colleague, and the reason why I was able to finish this book.

To Sumana Roy, elder sister and secret admirer.

To Namita Gokhale, for preparing me for this harsh, uncertain world.

To Arunava Sinha, Kapil Malhotra, Shobhaa De, Ravi Singh, Rupa Bajwa, Devaki Khanna, Meena Kandasamy, Abdullah Khan and Anees Salim for their handholding.

To Vineetha Mokkil, my gutsy editor for believing in the book and accepting it.

To my mother and father for always being there for me.

Part I
Ash

Dear Sonny,

I tried killing myself again and failed again.

I am writing to you from the hospital. My room is smaller and looks more run down than it was eight years ago. I don't know why my parents chose to admit me here when proximity is no longer an issue. The Army hospital is just opposite our house and now my father knows many retired Colonels and Brigadiers who supply him Blenders Pride at subsidised rates. Perhaps it has something to do with a mother's superstition – the hope that the hospital that saved her son from harm eight years ago would do it once again. One night, I even heard my mother telling my father how angry she was at herself for bringing her son to such a place.

The room is narrow, the ceiling low. There is a small window at the back. The glass is splattered with bird shit. Some deranged lover has scribbled 'Shruti – you mine only' across the wall in what looks like blood. A rod is fixed above the window from which hangs an old, brown curtain that has been tied up into a knot. God knows what manner of dirt, muck and strange creatures it is going to unleash if untied. As a result, in the afternoons, the sunlight streams through the windows leaving a round puddle of piss yellow near the door. At night, the room turns a rocky blue, the moon's soft, eerie light mingling with the darkness, interrupted only by the faint bathroom light that burns through the day.

The visitors have to request the attendants to provide them plastic chairs when they come to see patients. There are no sofas or chairs. The side tables are broken, the drawers jammed or full of the rejected paraphernalia of earlier patients. The *Hanuman Chalisa*, get-well-soon cards, notes scribbled in delirium, unused bottles of feel-good tonics and vitamins – all reminders of an illness they wish to forget and leave interred here.

The air conditioner has been replaced by a water cooler that spits out a hot, noisy blast of air. Every hour, the nurse requests a shabbily dressed man to come inside and fill the cooler with cold water from a hose. Shadowy figures of things that were integral to this room eight years ago swirl in the air and float around the corners of my weary eyes. I feel stupid and odd for wanting a sofa on my left, a small television fixed on the wall facing the bed, a refrigerator full of mineral water bottles and juices on my right. The shrieks of pain, present even eight years ago, are fewer and far between. The food tastes like warm water: the main course, salted water; the dessert, sweet water.

At first I thought I was hallucinating. But my doubts about the hospital being the same one I had been admitted to eight years ago were confirmed by one of the police officers on duty at the Mobile Police Post inside the hospital premises. I had been under observation for a deep wrist slit – the kind that we would have excitedly taken pictures of and seen again and again to lessen our pain – for three days and wanted to get some fresh air. I staggered out only to find one hospital attendant, one sweeper, and two police officers. One of the police officers was sitting inside the van, noting down the details of a crime scene. I don't know what warmed the other officer up to me. Was it the effortlessly melancholic look on my face, which, in hindsight, I feel was the first thing you noticed in me? Or the ineptly wrapped padding of cotton, gauze and bandages around my wrists, and the pain that made me hold my hands out like a beggar? Whatever it was, he asked me how I was feeling and I confided in him my misgivings about the place. The officer chuckled familiarly, as if I'd said something he had heard many times before. He was quiet for a moment, and then pointed his finger over the crumbling boundary wall to the right. He started talking about a new, state of the art, private hospital a few blocks away that had opened around seven years ago and had poached upon all the patients who used to come here. To further his point, he took me on a walk around the hospital, showing me a pharmacy with its shutter down, a once bustling canteen that had been replaced by a woman who had started selling tea and home-made biscuits on a wooden table, two ambulances parked under a shed that had been out of use for the last five years, one bathroom where 'even a stray dog won't go and shit', and the pitifully meagre offerings of coins and currency notes beside a tall statue of Shiva encased in glass. We walked back to the entrance. The officer saw me in the glare of full light for the first time, with an air of surprise. He softened his tone and asked me if I didn't mind telling him why my parents had admitted me to such a hospital. I told him the reason. He pressed my shoulder in a gesture, I guess, of understanding or sympathy, and walked briskly towards the van.

I had lost faith in the destructive powers of pills and hanging is too much physical exertion for me. So, this time, I simply decided to bleed myself to death. Sadly, I became unconscious after losing a lot of blood and was discovered by my mother. Here, at the hospital, they are replacing all the blood I had managed to lose. My father, mother, her sister, and her B-positive friends have all donated blood to save me. I cringe at the thought of all this incompatible fluid flowing through my veins. I wonder if this is going to make me a hybrid of all of them – inert like my mother, drunk like my father, a social butterfly like her sister, a braggart like her friends. I also wonder why some people can't let go of others.

There have been very few visitors these past few days. I don't think it is because of my parents' hesitation to inform people about my act, but for the simple reason that friends and family tend to lose interest in a mad relative who, they convince themselves over time, is destined to live a long life.

I remember the first day I was discharged from the ICU, eight years ago, as vividly as a mother remembers her first born. My parents were napping on the large sofa after three days of pacing up and down the ward. Suddenly, the door was flung open and five friends from school, two of whom I didn't even recognise, walked in holding bouquets of flowers, cards, and music CDs. Later, they would tell me that one of them had been feeling bored at home and so decided to come along, while the other was a girl who wanted to become a psychologist and didn't want to miss the opportunity of this real life 'case study'. Akki was the only one who came up to me and sat beside me on the bed. The rest sat on the sofa, yapping away about trivial things. He was also trying to cheer up my parents and make them remember the times when there was such a thing as a 'happy Ash'.

I don't remember the last time I was happy except in your company. And that is something no one knows, except the two of us.

The atmosphere turned almost festive with the arrival of my mother's sister, who brought leftovers from her son's birthday party and treated everyone except my parents and me. Aunt Pranita talked about her school and college days, her first crush, her job, her two children, and her husband. The first thing she did when my father woke up was walk up to him and whisper in his ears, loud enough for everyone to hear, 'Didn't I tell you he was a bomb waiting to explode? A vegetable for life?'

My father bit his lip and went to the bathroom. Four of my 'friends' left, promising to come the next day – they never did. Akki stayed back.

I swear that I never deliberately tried to hide my real name from you. I have always been fond of short names. That's the reason I call all my pets – two dogs, a turtle, a goldfish – by names of less than five letters. During our time on the rooftop, I wanted to share my real name but I really love the ring of Sonny and Ash together. Say it to yourself. Sonny and Ash. Now say it again.

Sonny and Ash.

I know that Akki's arrival, during our escapade at the hotel, must have come as an unpleasant surprise to you. Two days before this attempt, I tried calling you but you never took my call. I even stood outside the gate of your house at the time of our morning walk, but I didn't see you or Madaan, or even the girl. I guess seeing Akki and me together must have been too much for you. I realised that I was alone again. And to kill this loneliness – I wasn't sure, then, whether I possessed the strength to kill myself – I decided to find out whether we had left a legacy.

I visited Sriganesh Garden first. It was just like the time the two of us had gone there, but all the couples, whom I noticed making out in secret nooks and corners, had covered their faces with towels, shawls and even children's masks. After that, I went to the pub, RGP, in Vasant Lok. At the counter, there was a security guard body-checking everyone thoroughly. It was the same at Future Zone in Hauz Khas. Satisfied, I went to GR Hospital and enquired about the young man who had attempted suicide. I learnt that he never made it and died a few days after we had left him. I came to know how the late Mr Kumar's younger son was sent to jail after his fiancée's father lodged a complaint with the police about the dowry. I went to P Bazaar too but could not find the boy selling belts. I don't know if you remember, but you left Ellen's business card at the coffee shop of Hotel Le M One night, I decided to call her up. I introduced myself as the boy whose mother had met her at the hotel and told her about her three sons. She became hysterical and said that she didn't want to speak to any Indian or talk about India. I instantly disconnected. Our plans had all worked perfectly.

I know that we might never meet again and that you have the right to be angry with me. I will really miss the times we had together.

Yours,
Ash

Part II
Sonny & Ash

Chapter 1

Sonny meets Ash a little after 11 am.

She had beaten up her seven-year-old maid after a violent argument with her husband over their two sons. Later, when the little girl turned up outside her bedroom door with a bruise on her lower lip, she gave her an old bottle of nail polish and lip gloss to distract her. The maid is the asylum of flesh and bones in which Sonny often seeks refuge. She is also an expert at convincing her dying mother-in-law that what she is eating – usually sliced potatoes with a mild garnish of salt, pepper and the strongest sleeping pill Sonny can get her hands on – is different from what she ate a while back.

Sonny is already irritated by her sister-in-law's presence in the house and the way she had elaborately narrated her dream over dinner. She spent the entire morning brooding over it, so much so that she even forgot about the highlight of her day. She doesn't like being late for her daily pilgrimage of hate with Ash. Her fists are still pulsing from the blow to her maid's lower lip. She will strike her on the upper one as well if the gloss doesn't adequately hide the bruise – to give the whole pout a uniform distension.

She doesn't want her husband, Madaan, to know that she has an emotional safety valve in her young, orphaned maid.

Sonny is old enough to be Ash's mother. But unlike mother and son, this pair is bonded by their love for hating almost everything. They usually choose this hour as all the men are in their offices and the women are busy with their daily chores. More significantly, because Ash's brother has also left for office and his mother is busy cleaning up his father before throwing him to another pointless day of existence.

She is late by ten minutes.

Ash doesn't know how to express his anger. Rather than saying anything, he punches himself hard on his thighs. When he can't feel enough pain, he clenches both his fists and knocks the knuckles hard against one another.

'That's better. I must not harm myself. I have to live for my father.' When the signal doesn't reach his brain, he repeats, 'I have to live for my father.'

He makes sure that Sonny does not notice him. She is striking an ivory-handled cane on the ground. Her sweater pockets are bulging with odd shapes. She taps him on his shoulder.

'Don't you see anything unusual?'

Ash doesn't say a word, turns around and starts walking. She races to catch up with him, when she sees an old man across the road. He is slouching behind the fencing installed before the boundary wall of the old Army hospital, pissing and heaving a sigh of relief. Sonny crosses the road, picks up two bricks lying in a heap of garbage and burnt leaves next to the road, and mounts them in front of the small vertical space in the fencing. She feels jubilant and basks in the glory of this accomplishment. Now he'll have a tough time getting out. You can't do things so easily. You can't escape when people like me can't I had such a difficult day and it's barely noon. Why should he feel so relaxed?

The old man looks at her with an embarrassed smile. Sonny wonders how he can smile now. She looks at him, then back at the two bricks. Why isn't he noticing the obstacle? Is he trying to pretend that I don't exist? Do people ignore difficulties? Is that a way to escape from them?

She responds with a smile. But when he turns back to zip up his trousers, she adds two more bricks to the tower of her hate. She is not happy with the result. But she hopes he has a difficult time. Like she always had.

Ash stares at the bright yellow coat of paint on the army tenant's quarters on top of House Number 6. He remembers the house because of their driver who ran over a litter of abandoned pups for two consecutive days while reversing the cars out of the driveway. Their limbs were so frail that they couldn't move and the driver had parked the car in such a way that, when he reversed, the tires went right over their bodies. The pups cried for their mother, meeting their fate one after the other.

Are army men paid well? Ash wonders. It's not even festival time Then why have they painted the house? Do they have so much spare cash?

Ash squirms when Sonny walks back and catches up with him, breathing heavily. She is stocky, but her height saves her from seeming obese. She wears loose, baggy pyjamas and a white kurta, with an extra-large Nike or Reebok T-shirt, which her son used to wear to the gym, over them. She completes this odd look by wearing thick-rimmed spectacles and a pair of grey Adidas shoes. In contrast, Ash is lanky, his hair falling all over his round face, his eyes droopy and drugged, his walk unsteady. He is wearing track pants, flip-flops and a T-shirt with 'cult' printed on it in gold.

They have just started their walk when Sonny notices a sparkling new Chevrolet standing regally next to House Number 10's old Honda Accord. Are they that rich? She wonders.

'Let me check the number plate. I'm sure it's not theirs.'

'Forget it,' Ash says, but a large part of him wants her to check it.

A dark-complexioned man, with keys dangling from his finger, accosts Sonny. Sonny turns her jealous gaze away but Ash motions her to confront him.

'Whose car is this?' she asks.

'It's my boss's,' he replies tersely.

Sonny is not satisfied with this information. It won't give her the necessary social ammunition to get back at them. Knowing whether this car belongs to them would give her a better idea about their bank balances. For the last year, this particular neighbour's old Honda Accord has been her only solace when she looked at her own two second-hand cars. She tried her best to ask their maid if she could find out whether they were paying for their purchase in installments (knowing that they were still not the legal owners of the car would have brought her even greater comfort).

All that the maid was able to disclose was that the couple had an eleven-year-old, recalcitrant son who had already decided that, when he grew up, he would buy a helicopter after selling this house and go to Manali every month. He is still being tutored privately as no school is willing to take his nonsense. The parents have told everyone that he is a genius who will work for NASA one day and will be the first Indian to walk on the moon. The maid also told her that when his elder sister got married, he raised hell till he was given money equivalent to that spent on the two functions and the dowry, and forced his broke parents into a cruise trip – to Singapore first and, then, to New Zealand. Sonny was ecstatic. 'Every house should have a son like this,' she had screamed in delight, handing the maid a crisp ten rupee note.

'I recently got booked by the traffic policeman for a wrong number plate. I want to see these new number plates just to make sure,' she tells the driver.

The driver doesn't know how to turn down Sonny's request. He must have been involved in several accidents, Sonny thinks. She sees a scar on his left cheek and wonders if it has been inflicted by a knife. She forgets the purpose behind approaching him and entertains this new fantasy – the driver with the permanently scarred face. Next time, when someone asks her why she doesn't have a driver and has to trudge through the crowded streets of Delhi on her own, she can cite this driver and say that they are a raucous bunch and will pick fights for small reasons. To an unbiased eye, it's clearly the small incision of a blade.

He shifts away from her while she is still thinking about his scar and how she could use it to make her web of lies more intricate.

'Go ahead. Look at it.'

It is a moment of suspense for Sonny.

Ash is thinking about the paint. Do army men earn big bucks? They've wasted their money anyway. The paint on the house looks terrible to him, even though his room is a similar bright yellow. Maybe the identical yellow. The weather and the pollution must be turning it a different colour, he thinks. No, it's not the same as that of my room. He wrestles with his conscience, or whatever is left of it.

Going behind the Chevrolet to check the number plate, Sonny prepares herself for yet another defeat. Years of fruitless existence have made her a pessimist.

Suddenly, voices are heard from behind the main gate. Sonny doesn't want to be embarrassed. Facing the car, she sees the initial 'HR' instead of 'DL' on the number plate of the Chevrolet. She feels victorious and nods joyfully at Ash.

The two are walking side by side in the strong breeze.

Sonny wants to get closer to Ash but she doesn't know how he will react. They speak very little, but at times this silence generates a telepathy of conversations.

She wants to know why Ash attempted suicide. After all, she had come to know about him when the doctor at the hospital in Naraina had consulted her husband after the lavage was completed. Madaan was so excited that there had been a suicide attempt in the neighbourhood. 'Now, I'll have a permanent source of income. These suicidal bastards hardly get over their medication'. He advised the most potent medicines for Ash which led to severe headaches and stomach trouble – all so that he could make some extra money. After Ash was discharged, his mother had stopped buying medicines from Madaan Chemists and so Sonny doesn't know what he's taking. If they are the same medicines, he must see a new doctor.

'Please, Ash. Talk to me. I'll give you the names of medicines that have hardly any side-effects.'

Years later, she saw a pallid yet beautiful boy walking in the field with his two dogs. She hadn't been able to take her eyes off him. One day, she simply stood outside the new post office building and waited for Ash to approach her. He did. He told her that he felt very lonely and wanted to have friends in the colony. But he never talked about his suicide attempt.

'I don't know,' was all that he said when Sonny had questioned him. 'I was very gregarious in school. I don't know what happened after I gained puberty.'

'What?' she had asked.

'I don't know.'

She was afraid of losing him. Still, she wanted to know the cause of his aloofness and he continued to evade her.

They see barricades, checkpoints and maps for the defence area after turning right from House Number 20. Suddenly the road turns smooth and more even. Sonny rubs the cane on the road to feel it. She starts talking about Madaan. His shop is in the low profile Mansarovar Garden in West Delhi. When people ask her where he works, she is enraged. She starts hating him for being a middle-class chemist and making her responsible for two unsuccessful sons. But she tempers her hatred because, as much as she would like not to, she has to live with him.

'Okay, so tell me the details,' Ash says.

'Twenty packs of condoms – five small-sized, three flavoured, rest regular,' she replies. 'A lot of Viagra,' she adds as an afterthought.

Ash is upset. He can't believe that people he doesn't know are still having sex.

'Did they smirk when they asked for it? Did they say whom they were taking them for? Did they look well off? Did they pass a naughty comment? Crack a lewd joke?'

'No, I can't ask my husband all that. He'll grow suspicious. He tells me all this, happy that I'm still interested in sex.'

'So what does he do then?'

'Nothing. He simply asks me to rub some of my juices on the faces of models and actresses in *Femina* and *Cosmopolitan* and runs to the bathroom.'

'What about you?'

'I am too depressed to think about sex.'

'Good,' Ash rejoices. 'Nobody has sex. You are no different.'

'So, how is your mother-in-law?' Ash asks, as they cross a twisted heap of metal on a pedestal of stones. It must mean something to the army men. Sonny hopes that it is a piece of wreckage from a war. And that everyone in the accident or crash died.

'She is not dying. I am very worried. I have consulted all the priests at the local temple and all of them are of the opinion that she should die in a month's time. But that hag just doesn't go! My sister-in-law had a dream. God told her to make her mother visit the elder son in London – to attain salvation. She even narrated the dream to my husband while we were having dinner. Madaan was convinced that this was a dream from god. What are we going to do Ash? We can't afford a nurse, let alone a vacation in London for a mad old hag. She is saying that her mother's spirit will haunt us if we don't act on her dream. I am sure the bitch wants to expose our financial condition.'

Ash just nods and Sonny swings the cane angrily in the air.

It is winter, so the stray dogs have set up ways to survive the weather. The earth in the sewer is moist from the previous day's unexpected shower. A bitch has burrowed out a hole for her newborn pups. They are huddled together – leaping, sliding, and brushing off one another's fragile bodies.

Ash wants to go back home to his two dogs. Sonny remembers her own small Pomeranian who was stolen from her house. After that, she couldn't sleep for months and asked Ash to visit her home so that he could write letters to her relatives and draw 'Missing Dog' Posters. When Madaan refused bounty money for Jerry, she took off one bangle from her dying mother-in-law's hand and sold it. When he asked her where she had arranged the money from, she told him that it was Ash's. The dog was never found. Since then, dogs were included in her long hate list.

She takes a diversion from their walk. When the guard at the Military Engineering Services office, which they've left behind, stops a car for identification, she swings her ivory-handled cane at the bitch. The bitch screams and runs back into the hole. Sonny feels mildly satisfied. Tomorrow it will be the pups' turn. One gentle swing on their backs will suffice. Or maybe she could go closer and press the cane on their tiny tails. She can do whatever she likes, but she must be careful not to kill them. She simply wants to make their life more miserable. After all, she is suffering so much.

The wind has grown stronger. Sonny takes out a handkerchief from her pocket and wraps it around her head in two tight knots. She can feel a migraine coming.

They cross a huge electric pole. This is a landmark for them, as the row of off-white army quarters starts from here. These are small single-storied houses with the porticoes allowing space only for an armchair or, sometimes, a couple of chairs. Some of them have bamboo fences that hide gardens with beautiful hedges and artistic landscaping. Sonny stands in front of the small gate of the first house they cross and peeps through the window. She sees amber-coloured light filtering through.

'This means they have electricity. They have electricity twenty four hours a day, while our colony's transformer burns every other day. Do they realise that it only adds to my difficulties when I have to eat cold food and do without the heater?'

She sees an electric wire dangling from the top and remembers how she used to dispatch her servant after midnight to snip all the wires. On one such occasion, he was electrocuted and he died. All that was left of his attractive face was peels with patches of exposed light pink flesh, black scratches and burn marks. Sonny refused to recognise him. 'He must be from the slums,' she had said. When his parents came to her house all the way from the Kumaon Hills, she told them that he had left. Her husband, who hated more selectively, gave them Rs 5000 without her knowledge. But he did hide the truth from them.

While their son's remains lay in a cemetery, the two parents set off on a frantic search for him. Sometimes, they came back, defeated. But Sonny would always be too busy. She would beat up her seven-year-old maid if she opened the door for them, even though Madaan had allowed them to use the quarters for freshening up and making themselves a cup of tea. With no righteous way to kick them out, she had stashed the maid's undergarments in the old, half-blind father's suitcase and created a scene when Madaan returned from work. He had no choice but to politely ask them to leave and never come back.

'How strange,' she said before going to sleep. 'What is this world coming to? Was he here to find his son or molest an innocent seven-year-old? For heaven's sake, he can't even see properly.' Madaan didn't know where the truth lay so he simply listened till Sonny, exhausted by her theories and fabrications, fell asleep.

They reach the mess office. Someone is wiring lights on to a tree. She hurls an expletive at him. At night, bands will play

Police and Bryan Adams and the sound will drum in her head because of the defective speakers.

'These poor people,' she spits out. 'How do they feel like celebrating when they can't even afford a holiday and have to go to deserted hill-stations and stay in army guest houses? When they send their juniors to sell petrol at Rs 30 a litre to garage owners or Scotch at a higher price to civilians after they've bought the discounted whiskey from the army canteen? How can they celebrate?'

Ash is not worried about the sounds of celebration. The only sounds that resonate in him are the staccato rhythms of typing, daily domestic squabbles and the gurgle of the toilet flush. Everything else is so rare and such a delight. Whenever the phone rings he becomes excited and gets an erection. He thinks one of his school crushes is on the line. He doesn't know whom exactly he had crushes on, but he remembers masturbating a lot when he was not self-medicating. He is least concerned about why Sonny is grumbling about the army men. He spots bartenders in black-checked cut-sleeve coats laying the plates and arranging the cutlery. His eyes dart straight towards their crotches that look like flattened Vs. He looks for one with a bulge, but sees nothing. Then, as if to neutralise the consequence of his glaring, he looks at Sonny and tries to be drawn to her pendulous breasts. He doesn't feel attracted. 'I am not gay. This is a plot. I am not gay,' he shouts.

'I know that,' Sonny says.

It's time to call her younger son, Vinod, who is doing his MBA in Bombay. It's a third-grade institute that attracts lowly public sector or loss-making enterprises at the time of internship. She tells everyone that it is ranked as one of the best MBA institutes in the country. 'Aren't those the IIMs?' people ask, if they have the temerity to stand up to her. 'No, no. Don't read the newspapers. They lie. You know it. It's the best institute because it is. Do you doubt me?' She tries to induce guilt. 'No,' the friend says and stays quiet.

The cell phone is ringing. Ash can't wait to hear a new sound. There is a voice message in a sloshed tone.

'Hey guys! This is Vinod from Mumbai. Cool, composed, and a killer for everything Cobain. Yes! The man lives long after he has died. And don't forget the oneliners when someone gets me drunk. Before leaving a message just remember to chill out. Yes. Chilling out is the most important thing in life. Have a beer, take a few puffs, or just lounge on a beach thinking about the most popular sport in the world. Sorry, guys. It's not soccer. It's sex! Don't take life seriously, dude. Just be cool like I am. You just get one life. Enjoy it and fuck whoever comes in your way. I am not at home right now. Leave a message and if it's cool, you might just hear my sexy voice...'

'Bastard,' Sonny shouts. 'Have we mortgaged the house for his chilling out?'

Ash doesn't have anything to say. The concept of chilling out sends a cool breeze inside his head. It's a new toy he can stare at and turn around till he is sick of it.

'Why couldn't he do well in the GMAT so that he could study abroad on full scholarship? Why now, when we have spent so much money on getting him into a third-rate college? Why is he acting like this?' Sonny shouts, disconnecting the phone.

They see crisp red table spreads on different counters at the official MES lawn where army men get high and make false promises of love – to both, hapless women and a hapless nation. Sonny wishes she could go inside and rub off her mascara on the table just so that a guest gets distracted while serving himself dinner.

There is a small cage full of balloons that young children will stamp on and burst, one by one. Beyond that is a makeshift stage with two speakers on either side. A young, handsome boy (Ash looks at his crotch and then back at Sonny's breasts) is fixing a wire on a switchboard. He has a steel-blue electric guitar next to him and a plastic CD case. Sonny wonders if all this is affordable. She is sure that the guitar has been borrowed from some rich man's son who is a musician and is studying at some university in a corner of the United States. Sonny has to be critical of an education in the States. 'It ruins their mentality and makes children drift apart from the parents,' she had once commented.

The voice message reminds Ash of Sonny's younger son's GMAT. She is disturbed that Vinod failed it. His English was very poor and he left the examination hall after reaching the 'logical reasoning' section. It baffled him and his head could not take the strain of looking at the choices. Sonny told everyone that he caught a cold as he was sitting right in front of an air conditioner. Sonny even called up old, forgotten friends and distant relations to explain Vinod's dilemma to them.

Ash had been at her place, filling up the stylised lettering in Jerry's 'Missing Dog' Posters with sketch pens. Sonny had taken one whole day to find the most expensive paper and another hour to choose the right combination of sketch pens that would look the most impressive. Ash understood this excess, but couldn't really relate to it. After all, any day could have been the death of Jerry. It probably had been. She had been hysterical and was dialling numbers, including international ones, at random, talking about

Jerry and Vinod's plight. She was also nodding at the wonderful work of art on which Ash was working assiduously.

'Jerry should be in a different colour. Red isn't all that great. Try green. It will look more impressive. Reduce the font size of 'Missing'. Increase the size of 'Jerry'. It is an attractive name. That way, people might think we are fashionable.'

Most of her friends and relatives never understood why she kept calling and, for one whole week, her husband was flooded with calls about his wife's well-being. He'd explain how much she had loved Jerry and that everything was because of the missing dog. Later, he called up Ash to thank him for his work on the posters.

Sonny chose to advertise her poster in the army veterinary at 5 pm because that was when the influx of pets and their owners was at its peak. She told Ash that she might even find some highly influential army man who could arrange for a seat for her younger son in a better college.

The two days when they were frantically searching for Jerry through the 'Missing Dog' Posters posted alongside mating ads in the veterinary hospital, one senior army man's black Labrador was being treated for partial limb paralysis. There was hardly any treatment. He was simply being fed and given fluids and the doctor was waiting for his condition to improve. Sonny's plans had failed as the gravity of this situation had overwhelmed that of her missing dog. So, in desperation, she added to the poster, 'I think he could be severely injured. There were trails of blood on the staircase soon after he vanished.' Her trick had only attracted the Colonel, who looked at the poster once or twice and wished her strength in this hard time.

'How much I hate these army men,' she had started reciting ever since.

They have reached the cobblestoned path near the main powerhouse. Crocodile-coloured army trucks are plying through. They are the big bullies of the Cantonment area. These army men like to swagger around in them, jumping red lights and staring at civilians harshly. They hate paying fines and sometimes even get into scuffles with the policemen who chase them after they've mowed down civilians with their trucks.

A group of young athletic jawans, wearing green vests and shorts, are jogging along. Half of them sleep with the other half. The other half has wives back home or deluded parents waiting for their manly sons to get married. Ash is too excited to pinpoint one of them and his glare loses its focus.

Army wives are out to pick up their children from the bus stop. They are wearing sports shoes and are walking with a swift, disciplined gait. Ash wonders about the shoes' brands while Sonny is ranting about how they are saving on fuel. 'They tire out the children after long hours of study by making them walk down from the distant bus stop,' Sonny shouts. 'They don't encourage sports. Just study, study, study.'

Most successful sportsmen are from the army. But Sonny doesn't like those sports. Shooting and *kabaddi* are too small. Who cares? I haven't ever heard of a shooter or a kabaddi player.

'So, what are you carrying in your pockets?' Ash asks.

Sonny is exultant. He has finally seen her act of rebellion.

'It's the perfumes my brother-in-law had gifted my father-in-law. They are too expensive and I don't want my sister-in-law to say that she has any right over them.'

'So what do you see for the hag, Ash?' she asks, finally coming to the most important point of today's secret conference.

'Alright,' he says. 'I think that your mother-in-law will die around the time you desire.'

'Are you sure?' she asks, specks of hope in her eyes.

'Yes. But then, will that change anything?' he asks.

'No, nothing.'

Chapter 2

Sonny has been waiting for him for over an hour.

It is around 10.30 am but the road is still barren except for the occasional patient returning from the Army Hospital, and rickshaw pullers riding their empty rickshaws after the passengers have alighted at the barrier next to House Number 1.

Sonny sees a huge antenna being fixed on the roof of House Number 4. She starts missing her old servant and is sure that, had he been alive, he would have managed to climb up the roof and disrupt the antenna just as easily as he used to snip the electric wires.

'Stop this,' she shouts.

A man starts staring at her. Sonny turns her face away and sees her old maid Shanti walking towards her. Sonny vividly remembers the day Shanti had been forced inside a speeding blue Maruti van by three drunken men and was raped repeatedly as they drove through the empty and unmanned roads of the defence area. After they were through, they had dumped a hysterical and bleeding Shanti outside Sonny's gate.

For two months, Shanti lived inside her servant quarters because her family and husband had abandoned her after the incident was reported in a Hindi daily. Madaan tried to reconcile her orthodox family to the situation, but they were not even willing to see her. After recovering, Shanti found her peace in helping Sonny with kitchen work and knitting sweaters for her two sons.

One day, Sonny was walking on the same road where Shanti had been attacked. Suddenly she had this strange urge to stand at the exact spot where the men had taken Shanti hostage and see if any car would even slow down, if any men would look at her. In two hours, at least twenty cars passed her including those driven by groups of young men. She even smiled coquettishly at the driver of a Maruti van thinking that it was the same car used by Shanti's rapists. When the driver didn't even look at her, Sonny was agitated and started feeling that maybe her maid was attractive and she wasn't and that was why the men had wanted to rape her. On her way back home Sonny felt a pang of jealousy towards Shanti for being able to sexually arouse three men even if they were all drunk. The next day, she drove Shanti out of her home saying that she was not much help and that she needed the empty quarters for a full-time servant. Today, she simply turns her back to her once beloved maid and waits for her to pass by.

Sonny is about to cross the road and hide behind one of the cars to wait for Ash when she sees a group of labourers returning early from work. The one in front is holding an old radio next to his right ear, lost in a Bollywood melody. Another is cleaning his teeth with a twig. The two at the back, the ones that are disturbing Sonny the most, are holding hands. Their clothes are soiled with dust, mud, cement and the stains of their meagre meals. The soles of their slippers have peeled off and flap at every step. The calm, almost oblivious bliss surrounding them is irritating Sonny.

She walks back to the boundary wall and squats. She looks around to see if anyone is watching her, then slowly pulls down her pyjamas. She sits there as if urinating till the labourer at the front catches a glimpse of her and almost falls. Sonny continues to squat, spreading her legs further apart, revealing her hairy crotch. The labourer says something to the ones behind and soon all of them are staring at Sonny. The radio is silent, the twig has been thrown away and the two gay labourers have stopped fooling around with each other. When their stares become too obvious, she simply turns her face away, opening and shutting her legs at regular intervals. One of the labourers at the back shouts something and soon all of them start walking fast, keeping their eyes fixed on the road ahead. Sonny gets up, slowly pulling up her pyjamas, gratified to have dispersed the group that seemed too happy to be true.

Sonny and Ash have started walking past the houses. They have just reached House Number 9 when Ash stops and holds his head.

'Anything wrong, Ash?'

'No. Just a headache.'

'Must be because you lost your job.'

'No. Not really. I didn't deserve that job in the first place. You can't head a content firm with no experience. Anyway, forget it Sonny. Can we please get on with our walk? Both of us need to shed some weight.'

'Oh, Ash! You're such a gentleman! *Some* sounds so reassuring.'

The two have just crossed the house when Sonny sees the owners of House Number 10, an old man and his middle-aged wife, open the latch of the gate and walk out. She pulls Ash by his sleeve and drags him behind House Number 9's Maruti Swift.

with long hair and stubble, instantly attracts Sonny and Ash's attention. Sonny is sure that he is gay and that is why it would be unfair to compare his looks with those of her two 'perfectly normal' sons. Ash can't take his eyes off him. The man is waving a small, crumpled chit at Ash. He can't believe that such a good looking man wants to talk to him.

As he walks towards the Tata Safari, Ash has already started imagining the man agreeing to getting whipped once for every step he takes towards the car. Whenever he flinches or evades the whip, he will take a step back. After all, Ash is not obliged to go and help a complete stranger like him. He will, therefore, have to bear the pain. To answer his question, the man will have to leave the car and follow Ash into a closed, dark room. Although Ash will be fully clothed, the man will have to take off his clothes. Ash will lie down next to him, put on a pair of gloves and stroke the man's stiffening penis. If he shuts his eyes in pleasure, Ash will slap him on his face. If he shouts, Ash will try to calm him down by stroking his penis again. If he looks ecstatic again, Ash will punch him hard on his thighs. Ash will give the man his answer only after he is visibly bruised and shaken. Then he will let him walk back to his car.

'How can I help you?' he asks the man.

'Dude, I'm lost. Is this Charan Singh Park, Delhi Cantt?'

Ash is about to tell him that it is when, suddenly, a woman pokes her head out of the car. She seems drunk and is falling all over the man, kissing and fondling him. Ash tries, but is unable to fit the woman into his fantasies. This makes Ash change his mind.

'I don't live here,' Ash says, looking at the chit. 'Let me ask my friend.'

He walks up to Sonny and shows her the chit.

'He is right in front of the house,' she laughs.

'Where?'

'Ash, this is Brigadier Singh's house. House Number 12, Charan Singh Park.'

Ash takes the chit away from Sonny's hand and makes a face before she guesses that he doesn't want to let the man find the house so easily.

'Did he insult you?'

'Yes.'

'How?'

'I can't tell you. It was very humiliating.'

'Then he will have to pay for it! Just go and stand in front of Brigadier Singh's nameplate. It clearly shows the house number and address. Let me deal with this bastard.'

'Alright.'

'Hi. I am Sonny. I'm afraid the house that you are looking for is not here. You will have to go left from here, right from the Kirby Place red light, and over two flyovers. You will then reach Janakpuri. Charan Singh Park is somewhere close to Janakpuri.'

'Oh God! Are you sure?'

'Yes.'

'Why? Is there a problem?'

'Actually, yes. This is Brigadier Singh's daughter. We met at a rave party last night and she got very high. Now she is stoned and only remembers her address but not the directions.'

'Sorry. No Brigadier Singh lives here. Now hurry up and leave. This is a high security army area. You don't want to get caught with a drunk woman here, believe me.'

'Thanks.'

Once they are outside House Number 14, Sonny covers her face with her left hand to avoid eye contact with the bitch and her litter whom she tortures in the mornings. Ash doesn't know anything about this.

Ash is about to go near one of them with a biscuit when Sonny shouts, 'Where did you get this Danish cookie?'

'It was lying on the pavement outside House Number 9.'

'Damn it. It must have fallen from my sweater's pocket.'

She looks at Ash, puts her hands in her sweater's pockets and takes out at least five Danish cookies in each hand.

'What are you going to do with these cookies?'

'Ash, my sister-in-law has come over to stay with us for two days. I begged Madaan not to let her inside but he said that he didn't have the heart to stop her from being with her dying mother. We don't let her use the kitchen. She has her breakfast and lunch at Shastri Bazaar and goes back to her house in Patel Nagar to have dinner with her husband before returning.'

'Sounds good to me. Where's the problem, then?'

'Tea time, Ash. She loves dipping biscuits, especially if they come free of cost, in her tea, which she prepares inside her mother's room using her personal electric kettle. Whenever she comes over to stay with us, I lock all our wafers, *namkeens* and biscuits in my almirah. But I had to get these Danish biscuits with me because I just couldn't risk my sister-in-law seeing them. She would start thinking that we are well-off and can afford to send her mother to London.'

'Is she that bad, Sonny?'

'She gobbled up a share in her father's small clinic knowing very well that we needed it more than anyone else. I can never forgive her for that.'

'Want one?' Sonny offers a Danish cookie to Ash.

'Can't resist,' he exclaims and takes a cookie from her.

The two have crossed the Kirby Place red light. On their left, just before the bus stop, two traffic policemen have stopped a truck and one motorcycle. Sonny whines about how everyone seems to be in a rush these days while Ash agrees with her. The truck driver is sitting still, waiting for one of them to walk up to him and ask him to step down, while the motorcyclist has already started arguing, frantically slipping out cards of 'influential people' from his wallet and dialling their numbers on his cell phone only to complain that they are busy.

If people riding motorcycles can have influential friends, then why can't I, with my two cars? Sonny wonders. But what if he is a rich man's son who loves riding motorcycles? She asks herself this uncomfortable question. No rich man would risk his son's life by letting him ride a motorcycle. But didn't one of Madaan's customers, a rich garment exporter, gift a Harley Davidson to his son on his eighteenth birthday? When her self-interrogation becomes too much for Sonny and her fragile world-view, she convinces herself that the man is a liar and must be dialling one of his relatives. Still, she is furious at her husband for not cultivating his rich customers and keeping their business cards so that she could also show off her influential contacts.

On the right, a woman is standing with her daughter outside the gate of the army school, negotiating with the guard, asking him to let her daughter in even though they are over three hours late. 'This is the discipline that the army parents are passing on to their children,' Sonny tells Ash. When the woman shows the guard her daughter's bandaged elbow, Sonny rants about the poor physical endurance of today's generation, reminding Ash how she never missed school even when she was suffering from a massive head injury. She is about to part her hair to show Ash the deep scar it left when Ash holds her hand and stops her. For the first time, Sonny feels that some trust is building in their strange association. However, before closing this topic, she does remind Ash to look at himself – a young, innocent twenty-five-year-old who is pumped with strong medications every day but is still able to join her for these healthy walks.

'This new generation is going to ruin our country's reputation,' she shouts.

'Yes, it will,' Ash remarks.

On the road next to the bus stop, empty but for an old man forlornly waiting for a ride, the two of them see fine glass strewn all over. Sonny starts fantasising about a major accident which, she is sure, involved a brand new car whose owner (a couple, in her fantasy) was driving it down to the Hanuman Temple to get it blessed by one of the priests (oh, the irony!) and a water tanker. Right now, she is unable to make up her mind about whether the tanker hit the car on its side or at the back. In the first case, the person in the passenger seat would have died immediately but the driver could have been saved. She is not sure whether it would be better to kill one person or both. If one is left behind then he'd live his life in pain and regret. But what if he finds another soul mate and forgets about the ex-lover in a couple of years? True love doesn't exist anymore, she tells herself before deciding what happens next. Finally, Sonny errs on the side of caution and decides that the tanker hit the car in the back, and the couple was hurled at the windscreen head on. She imagines a lot of chaos at the accident site – ambulances rushing the blood soaked, mutilated bodies of the couple to the hospital, the police arresting the driver of the tanker, terrified onlookers staring at the pool of blood, metal and glass on the road. If she had been there she would have told each and every one of them that this was what life gave you. That it was high time people started being aware of its inherent pain and suffering.

Ash starts remembering his childhood injury fantasy – while playing cricket in the field he had yearned to be hit by the ball so that all his brother's male friends would gather around him. While he lay there pretending to be unconscious, they would move their sweaty hands all over his face, trying to get him to regain consciousness. He would try his best to smell their palms or their hot breaths when they would bend down and beg him to say something. While being carried back home, Ash would brush his hands across their hair, their trembling lips, their underarms and sweaty chests. He was sure that he would not get caught because his friends would be too worried about him to bother about the slight movements of his hands.

Ash wishes that he was a part of this accident so that he could play out his injury fetish on a wider scale.

They snap out of their fantasies when Sonny sees the old man waddling towards a bus whose driver has stopped it way ahead of the stop.

'Wait. Wait,' the man shouts, clutching at his chest.

The two of them exchange glances and start walking faster. In a few seconds, Sonny starts running, leaving Ash behind to stand at a corner. The bus conductor is standing on the first step gesturing to the old man to hurry, while Sonny is trying to get within hearing distance. As soon as she feels that her voice will not get lost in the rumble of vehicles, she shouts, 'Excuse me. Your wallet has fallen.'

The old man continues to run towards the bus, when Sonny shouts again and grabs his attention.

'Yes?'

'You dropped your wallet while running.'

The man stands still, takes a deep breath, and is about to check his pockets when Sonny exclaims, 'You don't need to check! My son saw it falling out of your pocket. Please take it from him, she says, pointing at Ash, who is waving at the old man.

'I'll miss my bus.'

'Better than losing a lot of money.'

'Yes. That's true.'

The moment the man turns his back on the bus, it starts moving,

'But then again,' Sonny says. 'You're old and I don't want you walking down all the way to the bus stop to claim something that may not be yours.'

'But you said it fell out of my pocket.'

'Yes. But my son has a mental disorder. Sometimes he sees things.'

'Why didn't you tell me earlier?'

'I don't know. I didn't want a senior citizen like you to even come close to losing money.'

The man stops again. He puts his hand inside his pocket and takes out a black wallet. He checks the compartments, counts the coins, then looks at Sonny, disgusted.

'Why did you do this?'

'Do what?'

He turns back to see that the bus has left.

'I won't get a bus for another hour.'

'Do you feel bad?' Sonny asks, going closer to the man, peering at his crinkled face and protruding shoulder blades.

'Of course.'

'How bad?'

'Very.'

'Do you think I have been able to exercise control over your life?'

'What?'

'Nothing. I hope you find a bus soon.'

The two leave the man behind. Sonny thinks that this was a beautiful, real-life metaphor for difficult people and events pulling her back to the same place in life, while Ash just revels in the madness of the whole exercise.

They cross a sign pasted on a tree that says 'SAT, GMAT, GRE classes. Study in your favourite college abroad.'

Sonny takes out a handkerchief from her pocket and starts wiping the tears streaming down her cheeks.

'What's wrong Sonny?' Ash asks, comforting her by patting her back.

'Vinod's GMAT, Ash. I have discovered something very disturbing.'

'What?'

On their way to Shastri Bazaar, Sonny tells Ash how her son couldn't crack the GMAT because of the examination centre where the test was conducted. She told him that, had the test taken place at USEFI and not the American Embassy School, where there were enough American girls to distract a young, sexually aware boy appearing for his exams, he would have done well. She had herself seen how Vinod was staring at a group of foreign girls standing next to the gate and was sure that he was not able to get rid of their image during the exam. There is no other reason, she concludes, why, after six months of intensive tutoring, he could manage a score of just three hundred.

A few days ago, Sonny had gone there disguised as a journalist and when all the candidates were walking out after the test, she had found out that at least seven out of the ten boys she had randomly chosen were convent educated. She tells Ash how there might be a conspiracy behind the GMAT, with the examination authorities giving preference to co-ed educated boys over convent educated ones.

When he asks her why they would be biased against convent educated schools, Sonny says that the answer is a simple one – some feminist organisation in the US must be filtering the male candidates aspiring to go to America for their higher studies and must have disqualified convent educated Indians since everyone knew that they were shy and socially awkward. By having them appear for their GMAT at the American Embassy School, they were trying to make the boys be distracted by the pretty girls. 'Ash, this could be another era of racial filtering,' she says with a serious look.

'That could be true,' he says, reciprocating her grave look.

As they enter Shastri Bazaar, Ash sees two army men in uniform entering the newly opened Happy Coffee Day. He nudges Sonny and points to the entrance of the coffee shop.

'Ash! That's terrible! People who get eggs and butter along with their meagre salaries are now spending hundreds of rupees on a cup of coffee. I am sure these army men share our intelligence secrets with Pakistan.'

'Or maybe they smuggle weapons?' Ash suggests.

'Yes, Ash. That too.'

'Where is the STD booth?' Ash asks as they enter the narrow lanes full of ration stores and small eateries.

'I have a plan Ash.'

'What?'

'I have heard that Happy Coffee Day is suffering losses from this outlet. We must make the already demoralised staff feel worse. I want you to stand right outside the entrance and keep smiling at the staff and staring at the food counter so that they think that you are waiting for someone to join you to have a meal here. Once I come back after making the call, we'll get ourselves chaat papdi from the shop facing it and stand outside their entrance eating blissfully. We'll constantly stare at the staff and hope that they see us eating chaat papdi rather than their thick shakes and stale chicken sandwiches.'

'Sonny, you are brilliant!'

'No, Ash. I have just started getting back at people. Now go there and wait for me. Remember, keep smiling at the staff. We'll start eating right outside the entrance the moment those two army men, I am sure the sole customers there, have left. The staff has to be idle and demoralised to get the important message we are trying to convey to them – the fact that they are failures.'

'Bloody failures,' Ash shouts.

'Yes Ash. Bloody, bloody failures!'

Ash stands outside the entrance, staring at one of the waiters clearing up the table where the two army men were sitting. He sees him and flashes a pleasant smile. Ash can't see any pain or uncertainty behind his smile and turns to the cashier at the counter, who points Ash to one of the tables. Ash turns away but, after a few minutes, he starts staring at the cashier again.

The latter mimes opening the glass door for him, but Ash ignores him. This continues for a while, before the cashier points to the huge television screen on the wall as if to ask if something special on TV has caught his attention. Ash does not react. The cashier starts feeling awkward and calls the two waiters behind the counter. The three of them stare at Ash. Instead of staring at them, Ash starts staring at the food counter, standing on his toes so that he can get a better view of the items on the first shelf. One of the waiters starts walking towards the door, smiling affably, before Ash grimaces and starts walking away. On the way, he meets Sonny coming towards the entrance with two plates of chaat papdi in her hands.

'Is it empty yet?'

'Yes. The army men have gone.'

'So can we start our game?'

'Yes.'

The two spend the next fifteen minutes eating the chaat and staring at the staff randomly. When the three staff members lose interest, Sonny screams in delight and the noise travels inside. The cashier looks up at them again. Sonny picks up a papdi from the plate and puts it in her mouth while staring at him. He looks away, feeling uncomfortable and calls the two waiters again. After speaking to him, one of the waiters dims the lights in the café, walks out and puts the 'Closed' sign outside the entrance.

The two of them turn into the main bazaar. One video library and several grocery shops have been rented out to individual businesses or banks to start ATM facilities. Some shops have sold off a part of their space and invaded the narrow pavement, leaving little space for people to walk. Sonny is wondering whether the shopkeepers are getting enough rent and its effect on their social standing, while Ash has clenched his right fist and started hitting counters, tables, boards and refrigerators on his way to ease his sexual tension. Whenever they come across a congested space, Sonny steps down from the pavement on to the narrow road but Ash elbows into people, ignores their shocked looks, and continues to march on.

'Any news of Jerry?' Ash asks, stopping before an ATM.

'No, Ash. I just spoke to a pet psychic in the US and she has told me that he is alive but might be injured.'

'So what are you going to do now?'

'I don't know. I can only hope and pray.'

Just then, Sonny spots a man standing in a queue outside the ATM. He is knocking on the glass door. She walks closer to see a man dressed in an army uniform standing before the machine and arguing on the phone.

'I think he doesn't have any balance left in his account,' Ash says.

'Really, Ash? How do you know?'

'I just saw it on the screen when he moved aside.'

Ash makes space for Sonny as she peeps through the glass door to try and get a glimpse of the words on the screen. The army man looks at her and gestures to give him some more time. Sonny points her finger at something on the wall above so that the man moves from in front of the screen. He moves a little to his left and looks up and Sonny is able to see the words 'Sorry, no deposit.' She starts laughing when the man standing behind her pats her on the back and asks her to make way.

Sonny and Ash move away from the door but wait for the dejected man to step out. Sonny would like to speak to him and tell him not to feel bad, that she too has gone through many financial upheavals. She is hoping that he opens up to her and tells both of them the story behind the ATM deposit. If they like his confession and feel that he is also suffering a lot, she might invite him to join them for their morning walks. Sonny turns to to Ash to share her plan when she sees the man walk out of the facility, laughing on the cell phone. Sonny immediately changes her mind.

'Some people, they don't even realise they're suffering,' she tells Ash.

'Who?'

'The army man, Ash. He is laughing even though he doesn't have any bank balance.'

'Oh? That's really strange.'

'I know.'

The two are standing outside a gift shop when Ash announces, 'I'm done for today.'

Chapter 3

Sriganesh Garden is situated right opposite Station Road, a few hundred metres ahead of Shastri Bazaar in Delhi Cantonment. A pavement, which separates a narrow lane from the rest of the road, is built along its front. It overlooks a Hanuman temple before which buses frequently stop for the passengers to get a drink of water from the taps outside and briefly pay obeisance to their god, if the driver and the conductor permit. A rusted green board before the entrance clearly states that the garden is meant only for those 'who want to be close to nature' and that no cycles and dogs are allowed inside. The wide stone steps lead on to an unevenly landscaped garden, full of plateaus and wave-like undulations surrounding a deep pond at the centre. The garden is dotted with stone benches, tiny flower beds, short Asoka trees and tall lamp posts.

It is a favourite spot for students, lower-class couples enjoying a picnic with their families and workers from the nearby MTNL office in search of a spot for an afternoon nap. It is also the haunt of couples who settle down on the benches under the shade of the Asokas and make out with a vigour that depends on the time of the day.

'I am sure they mean stray dogs. No one in his right senses would have barred Jerry from entering any place,' Sonny comments.

'I think the owners are just jealous because they can't afford to keep dogs,' Ash says.

'Of course, Ash! Why didn't I think of that?'

Today the garden is teeming with people – men sitting on mattresses and playing cards, families enjoying a quiet lunch, students lying down on the grass with school books open before them, people using their helmets and bags as pillows, women protecting themselves from the sun with their chunnis or shawls, couples walking about desultorily, pausing briefly before a man selling chips, cold drinks and juices or by the flower beds. Three young couples are openly making out – two on a bench and one behind a small, hunchbacked tree.

At first, Sonny and Ash simply walk close to people and start kicking the grass beneath their feet in the hope that dirt will land on their clothes and food. When that doesn't work, because of the hard earth, they laugh out loud so that people are at least distracted and look back at them. And when they do, they stare at them coldly. If someone looks inquisitive, they stop, hold hands and keep on staring. Occasionally, some people get agitated and are about to confront them, but Sonny and Ash quickly move on to the next couple or family. They stomp on flowerbeds, turn one of the water hoses in the direction of a sleeping man so that he gets drenched and chase away squirrels with small twigs.

After a while, they start looking into the pond where the water is so still and muddy that one can use one's fingers to carve out words there. The surface is littered with dry, brittle leaves, stems, petals and packets of chips. Sonny is hoping that the naked body of a dead woman suddenly bobs to the surface so that the authorities and the patrons have a hard time explaining its appearance to the police. Ash just wants the pond to be full of crystal clear water and his broken family here, swimming together.

Just when they start walking back, Ash catches a glimpse of a man who has spread his legs so that his girlfriend can sit between them. He has covered her, neck downwards, in a shawl and is holding her firmly with both his hands. After pecking her neck, he slides his left hand under the shawl and inside her. His hand is moving in and out as the girl is giggling, at times letting out a soft yelp. Whenever the man applies more force to her insides, the girl shakes up. The man then slips his hand out and pushes her back to the ground. Ash imagines himself in place of the girl, being fingered in the same way. He decides that, unlike the girl, when the man becomes too aggressive with his privates, he will bite his arm or swing his head so hard that it hits his chest. Only when he calms down because of the pain, will Ash accept his apology and let himself be touched again. When he realises that he has fantasised about a man, he slaps himself hard on his thighs promising himself that this is the last time. Soon, Sonny sees the couple too and the two of them stare for a few minutes, constantly holding and letting go of their hands and reminding themselves of their shrivelled, dried up sexuality.

'Sorry,' Ash says when his hand mistakenly rests on Sonny's breast.

'It's okay, Ash. I know you didn't mean it.'

'Yes. I didn't.'

Sonny and Ash find a vantage point, from where they can see two out of the three couples clearly – a success rate of which both are inwardly proud. Sonny takes her handbag off her shoulders and takes out two small pairs of binoculars, two pepper sprays, a packet of condoms, some white hair gel, a Polaroid camera, a writing pad and two bottles of mineral water. She passes a pair of binoculars to Ash and the two of them start studying the couples.

Sonny is the first one to see how the woman sitting between the man's legs is secretly trying to reach for his penis by moving her hand behind her back. She hopes that it eludes her grip just as love and happiness have eluded her. Each time the penis slips out of the woman's hand, Sonny starts thinking of a rotten aspect of her life – her incomplete education, her arranged marriage to Madaan, two unintelligent kids, a meddling sister-in-law and, most of all, a mother-in-law who is defying death. When the woman gets a firm grip on it and starts feeling it along its length, Sonny shrieks, shaking her head. Before the woman looks back to see where the sound has come from, Sonny quickly puts the binoculars back on the ground and pretends that she is lost in deep thought. The moment the woman resumes, she picks up the binoculars and starts looking again.

Ash is busy looking at the couple seated on the bench, the woman lying with her head down in the small crevasse between the man's thighs. Every time, before lowering his head to kiss her on the mouth, the man teases her by saying something mischievous – probably to make her comfortable. The odd kiss, looking more like two sets of lips squashed against one another, lasts less than a few seconds and the woman turns her face away and starts looking around the park nervously, sometimes raising her hand to touch the man's cheek. The man starts laughing. The woman sits up and faces the man. They have a minor argument before she slowly slips into his arms and kisses him again. Ash can feel the tension inside his pants but he ignores it, certain that some negative force is trying to make him sexually excited and thus susceptible to physical intimacy. After staring for long periods, the two of them take a break together, sometimes talking to one another, or focusing the binoculars someplace else.

'Do you think these couples are married?' Ash asks during a break.

'No, Ash. Married couples have their beds to fuck each other. They don't need to come to a park and make out in the open. Oh! Look! The couple behind the tree is getting more intimate and I can see the girl's face very clearly. Take the picture now, Ash.'

'Okay.'

Ash is about to take a picture when a stranger accosts them. He is wearing a black sweater and denim trousers, and has a card in his hand. Ash immediately puts the camera down and looks at Sonny. She starts collecting her paraphernalia and putting it inside the handbag when the man speaks.

'You don't have to do that.'

'Why?' she asks.

'Because I also love watching.'

'Watching what? We are not here to watch or anything. Right, Ash?'

Ash hesitates a little before nodding

'It's okay. There's nothing wrong with it. Actually, I run a club for watchers like you. We meet every month and share pictures and stories from our visits to parks like these. It's a very liberating experience, since most watchers are perverted or sexually repressed.'

'I am not gay,' Ash shouts.

'I never said you were gay. I said perverted or sexually repressed.'

'We are nothing like that,' Sonny smiles, trying to control her rage.

'Anyway, here's my card. The name of the club is 'Watchers.' We watch at every place possible. From pubs, cinema halls, parks, shopping malls, to school toilets. In fact, we have two male members from a very big private school who have recently joined us. We are even planning to make a movie out of the clips we have collected over the years.'

'How many years?' Sonny asks.

'Five.'

Sonny is tempted to take the card but feels that Ash might distance himself from her if he finds an attractive man or a woman during one of their meetings. She realises that she will have to make these walks and visits more interesting if she wants Ash to stay. After all, how can a frustrated housewife compete with a whole organisation of sick people for a rare find like Ash? On their next walk, she might even ask Ash for a few self-improvement tips. She'll promise Ash never to do things he doesn't like. But the boy is so quiet and non-judgemental, she worries that he might not open up to her. She still doesn't know why he attempted suicide or why he likes being with her. But she also knows that it would be very difficult for her to make do without him.

'We don't want your card or to be a part of this sick organisation. We are here just to watch the surroundings.'

'With condoms and pepper sprays? I must say that you two are way ahead of us. We 'watchers' mean no harm to the people we spy on. But I think the two of you have sinister designs.'

'Please leave us alone,' she shouts.

'Alright. But feel free to call me the day you feel comfortable enough to accept yourself for what you are,' the man says, dropping the card in front of them, and leaves.

'The man was crazy,' Sonny laughs nervously.

'But he did find out what we were doing.'

'Yes. Only what we were doing. Not what we'll end up doing,' she sniggers.

Ash smiles and the two give each other a high five.

While Ash is clicking pictures, Sonny sees a couple wheel an old woman inside the park. Her head is stooped and her hands fall against the arms of the wheelchair. Sonny is sure that this is an elaborate plan hatched by one of her neighbours to make Madaan and her feel guilty for not letting her mother-in-law out of her room. Otherwise what would a senile, invalid woman achieve from coming to a park full of young people? The couple lifts the wheelchair from the sides to put it on higher ground and find a place under a small tree. The man holds the old lady steady and she points out a flower bed right in front of her. When Sonny sees her creased face break into a faint smile, she gets agitated. When she can't recognise the couple, she decides that they are trying to get the old woman to sign an ownership document. Nonetheless, Sonny convinces herself that she doesn't get her mother-in-law to the park because she is dying and not because she doesn't own anything.

Ash has started taking out the condoms and filling them up with a mixture of hair gel and water, closely resembling the colour and texture of semen. He passes them to Sonny who puts them in polythene packs.

'Are you sure we should do this?' he asks Sonny.

'Of course, Ash! We can't let the younger generation be polluted by these sick minds! And the authorities will take note only when they find these condoms strewn over their beloved garden.'

'No... I mean, what if we get caught?'

'No, we won't. The guards here are lousy.'

'Alright then... You looked a bit upset today Sonny. Anything you would like to share?'

Sonny looks at Ash and lowers her head. He moves closer to her and lifts her by the shoulders. She turns and burrows her head between Ash's thighs and starts narrating the morning's events.

While having his breakfast at around nine, Madaan thought he heard his mother muttering. When he went inside he saw the maid picking up the broken pieces of a bowl in which she had been feeding her porridge. When he asked her what happened, the dumb maid gestured that his mother had suddenly opened her dazed eyes, pushed the bowl away and started speaking. He asked her if she knew what she was saying only to see the terrified maid pursing her lips, reminding him that she couldn't speak.

Madaan immediately called his sister, Bela, who covered fifteen kilometres of congested roads in less than twenty minutes.

By then, Sonny had become curious enough to go into the room she usually entered only to carry her mother-in-law to the bathroom and give her a bath or to change her diapers while she was in bed. After sitting beside her for a few hours, both she and her husband lost interest and, feeling that the maid must have been trying to cover up her own mistake, they went to their room.

But Bela sat there, waiting for her mother to say something. Just when Sonny was about to rest for a while and Madaan was ready to leave for his walk, the two heard Bela scream. As they ran inside, they saw how Bela was hugging her mother and crying out loud.

'Say it again Mummy,' she cried.

'Nandan,' she said.

'Nandan who?' Madaan asked, stepping closer to his mother and holding her hands.

'Nandan,' she said again.

'Look Madaan. Didn't I tell you that Mummy always wanted to spend her last days with Pramod in London? Even in this terrible state, she is clearly expressing her wish to go to London.'

'It's 'Nandan', Sonny shouted.

'No Sonny. Mummy is saying 'London'. We must not delay any further and spend the rest of our lives in guilt.'

'No Bela. She is saying 'Nandan,' Sonny shouted.

'Who is Nandan?'

'Don't you remember Nandu? Our cook and your mother's caretaker. She must be missing him.'

'He was Nandu, not Nandan.'

'His real name was Nandan.'

'It's London, Sonny. Why would Mummy remember a godforsaken servant in her dying days, instead of her dead husband or her children?'

'Because she loved him.'

'I don't believe this Sonny. Anyway, I have recorded her saying 'London' on my cell phone and sent a voice message to Pramod. You two must not play with our sentiments any longer and arrange for your mother's passport, visa, and ticket soon.'

After Bela left, Sonny and Madaan had a confrontation. Although he too felt that their mother was taking Nandan's name, he wasn't sure if they should stop her from visiting her elder son in London.

'Bela had a dream. Now Mummy says something sounding so much like London. Why not let her die in peace there?'

'I am not going to let you spend our precious savings on this mad old woman,' she shouted.

'She's ill, Sonny,' Madaan protested.

'But not alive enough to feel the pinch that we would suffer if we spent money on her trip to London. And why don't you ask Pramod and Bela to arrange the money if they want her there? They are richer than us.'

'Because father had told all three of us that he was giving this house to me in return for taking good care of mother while she is alive.'

'You and your family politics,' she shouted and locked herself up in the bathroom.

'Ash, we don't have any money. On top of that, we have two sons who are going to feed on us like vultures.'

'Don't feel bad Sonny. Look at me. I am twenty five and fully dependent on my father.'

'But at least you had a job for three months.'

'Three months only. And I was miserable.'

The two of them are lost in their respective miseries before Ash sees the man sitting behind the tree moving the shawl away from the woman as she hurriedly pulls up her pyjamas and smooths out the heavy creases on her clothes. She looks back at him and starts rubbing her forehead on his chest. He holds her with one hand and his erection with the other. A gardener looks at them while watering a bed of pansies on their left. The two of them reluctantly stop feeling each other up – the woman getting up on her knees, the man slowly sliding up against the twisted branch of the tree. They are almost ready to walk towards the exit when Ash waves at them. Sonny has stood up by now and is also looking at the couple.

The man sees Ash and shrugs, when Ash picks up one of the photos and starts pointing his finger at it. Although the man has still not understood why Ash wants to speak to him, he walks towards him, the woman closely following behind.

'Yes? Why were you waving at me?'

Ash shows him two photos of the couple making out behind the tree.

The man's face turns red while the woman starts panicking.

'What do you want?' he asks, holding the woman's hand.

'Meet us in the common bathroom and don't try to run or hide. We know the woman's phone number and home address. One mistake and we'll spill the beans,' Ash says coolly.

The man takes the woman to a corner. She is shivering and inconsolable but he tries to talk her into Ash's plan. A few minutes later, the two come back to Sonny and Ash and tell them that they are ready to do anything in order to get the pictures.

'Alright,' Ash says.

'Yes, fine,' Sonny adds. 'Wait,' she says holding up the polythene pack full of condoms.

'Yes?'

'Quietly scatter these at different places – not easily visible ones – on your way to the bathroom.'

'What are these?'

'Just do as I say.'

'Okay.'

Sonny and Ash are walking on the narrow walkway winding round the garden. They stand before the dargah of a Muslim saint, made of green tiles and canopied in shimmering cloth, right at the edge of the garden. Sonny sees a man standing near them, his head covered with a white handkerchief. He takes off his shoes and begins to wash his hands under a tap in the garden.

'Bloody terrorist coming from a dirty race!' Sonny screams.

The man locks up at her, still bent and washing his hands. Sonny continues to stare at the dargah, pretending that she hasn't said anything. She gently nudges Ash to see if she has startled the man. He looks back only to see that the man has shut his eyes and is reciting a prayer. He gestures to Sonny to see for herself and, when she does, she sees him looking straight at the dargah with his eyes shut.

Sonny looks carefully at the dargah to see if it can give rise to the same passion in her, but it doesn't. Instead her mind starts wandering to how a veteran maid of the colony had told her in the morning that House Number 2's owner was fighting with his son every day over a loan of fifty lakhs that he had given him two years ago to start his own business. She finds the possibility of a rift in the family very thrilling.

'Ash, how can a tomb make one so peaceful?'

'I don't know Sonny.'

'Isn't it convenient to pray after you have killed innocent people?'

'You mean he is really a terrorist?'

'Oh come on, Ash! All Muslims are either terrorists or have terror links. Thank God Gaurav is no longer going out with that Muslim girl from Pune. Who knows, she might have convinced him to blow up a building or something.'

'Why did he leave her?'

'He came to know that she had had an abortion and didn't tell him about it.'

'His child?'

'No, Ash! Please don't terrify me,' Sonny shouts, imagining a foetus with a long, wet beard on his chin and a bomb nestling between his legs.

The two are still looking at the dargah, when the couple looks out of the bathroom and the man waves at them. Sonny and Ash leave the serene Muslim devotee at the dargah and walk past the small, open nursery lined with flower pots, some of which are empty.

Standing outside the bathroom, the two of them watch the man standing before a urinal and the woman holding on to a small door on the right. Water is running freely from a tap, in the muck-encrusted wash basin. A broom with wet bristles is standing inverted next to the urinal. The floor is littered with matchsticks, cigarette stubs, tobacco pouches and wet, crushed tissue papers. The whole bathroom reeks of fresh and stale urine – an astringent smell that swirls around the edges of the nostrils.

Sonny enters the bathroom and the couple makes way for her. She pushes the woman aside and checks to make sure it is empty and doesn't have anything that the duo can use as weapons. She steps out and gestures to the man to turn off the tap and hand over the broom to her. She passes the broom to Ash who is outside. He stacks it against the wall. The man is trying to hold his own while the woman is visibly shaken, too afraid to look Sonny in the eye.

Sonny gestures to the woman to leave the door and stand next to the man.

'Take off your clothes,' she says.

'What?' the man shouts.

'No. Not you. You just take off your pants. She has to be completely naked. Now hurry up!'

Meanwhile, Ash is standing outside, with one eye on the scene inside and the other looking out for visitors to the bathroom. Sonny has instructed him to tell everyone that the bathroom was being cleaned and the floor was flooded with water. So far, no one has come this way.

The woman has taken off her kurta but looks reluctant to undo her bra and pull down her pyjamas. The man is naked waist down, squeezing his penis between his thighs.

'You sit down on your knees and face your girlfriend. And tell her to take off all her clothes before it is too late.'

'Please let us go. We were here just for some fun. There is nothing serious going on between the two of us. My father is a strict and unforgiving man and he won't let me breathe if I get caught,' the woman begs, sobbing.

'Take off your clothes. Hurry up!' Sonny shouts, hitting the wall on her right.

When all is ready, Sonny asks the couple not to move, goes out, and asks Ash in. She is hoping that he is impressed by her plan.

When the two walk inside, Ash is shocked to see the man on his knees, masturbating to a fuzzy printout lying before him. The girl is sitting on all fours, her nipples nearly touching the dirty, urine washed floor. Ash moves a few steps forward to see that the picture is in fact Jerry's 'Missing Dog' poster.

He looks at Sonny. She is waiting expectantly for a response.

'What, Ash? A young, unemployed loser like him must have wanted my little Jerry. Now he can have him!'

'Madam, I work with an IT firm,' the man interjects.

'Oh, please!'

'Let's go ahead with this,' Ash says trying to keep his apprehension in check.

'Oh, Ash! Thank you.'

Just then, Sonny sees how the man is distracted and looking away from Jerry. She looks at the woman. 'Do what I said. Your boyfriend is making life harder for you. I told you you'd have it if he stops looking at my lovely Jerry even for a second.'

'Please madam. Give us the pictures. I swear I'll never come to the park with a man again. Not only that, now I don't even feel like getting married.'

'Marriage is terrible, woman. Ask me. Anyway, now do what I told you.'

The woman bends her head and lets out a bark, wiggling her arse.

'Lick the floor,' Sonny says.

She sticks out her tongue and licks the floor.

The man sees her and immediately looks back at Jerry's picture and starts masturbating.

'Look away from the picture and she'll have to bark and lick the floor again,' Sonny says, breaking into a laugh.

After the man has ejaculated, Sonny asks the couple to stand up and huddle together in a corner. They obey her at once, the man standing sideways facing the corner of a urinal and the woman covering her crotch with her palms.

When the two point at their clothes, Sonny tells them to hold on.

She starts picking up their clothes from the ground and stuffing them into her bag.

The man protests. The woman swoons. He grabs the body of the naked woman and sets her down in a corner.

Just when Sonny is about to lift the handbag, Ash sees the man heading towards Sonny with a clenched fist.

'Sonny!' Ash shouts.

Sonny takes out a pepper spray from the bag and sprays it all over the man's face. He covers his eyes with his palms, screaming.

'Ash, let's lock them inside.'

'What about the pictures, Sonny?'

'Oh, yes!'

The two lock the bathroom door from outside. Sonny takes the pictures and scatters them near the door. Then, they quietly make their way to the entrance of the park.

'This was scary,' Ash says.

'Scary things happen to both of us all the time,' Sonny says casually.

Chapter 4

The two have reached Vasant Lok one hour ahead of time.

Sonny asks the driver to stop the car right in front of the entrance even though it is prohibited and the vehicle blocks the heavily congested road. The driver tries to protest but she reminds him that she is his employer and not the other way round. She is about to step out and join Ash at the security check when she sees a middle-aged man honking, poking his head out of the window and shouting at her.

She sits on the edge of her seat, bends down and pretends to strap her sandals. The man starts honking furiously, jumping up and down in his seat. Sonny alternates between staring at the man with a disparaging smile and fiddling with the strap of her sandals. The man moves the car forward with a sudden jolt but Sonny is undeterred. The driver looks back and asks if she could hurry up. Sonny raises her right hand asking him to be patient. The man brings his hand down on the steering wheel. Sonny gets up from the seat for a second just to give him false hope and, when he puts the car into gear, she sits down again. Just when the man is about to step out of the car and confront Sonny, she jumps out, shuts the door behind her and runs towards Ash. On her way, she looks at the long line of cars and scooters she has left behind. Her heart swells with pride and, for a moment, she feels important, superior.

The two are about to walk past the security check when Sonny sees a poster with pictures of four criminals pasted on one of the barricades. On top, scribbled with a black sketch pen, are the words:

'Notorious Murder Cum Robbery Bunty Gang'

Sonny stops right in front of the poster and looks carefully at the four men in the pictures. Two faces have already been scratched beyond recognition. Still, Sonny is worried that someone might identify the remaining two criminals – the one in the jeans and the kurta pyjama – and, with their arrest, her secret fantasy of her sister-in-law being robbed and cudgelled to death may never come true. She doesn't turn around when Ash hands over a sharpened pencil to her. She is happy that he fully understands her and her pain. She looks to her left to see a couple browsing through a glossy magazine and to her right, a police officer half-asleep inside a booth, then quickly stabs the pencil tip into the left eye of one criminal and drags it across his face. She does the same to the last criminal's picture and heaves a sigh of relief when she steps back and sees that the two pictures are now equally unrecognisable.

'They are coming for you Bela,' she screams in delight.

'Yes, they are!' Ash exclaims.

The two walk past the security check and decide to sit on a small bench outside McDonald's with a plastic clown angled to their right. Ash snuggles close to the clown and starts pressing his palm hard against its thighs. He turns to look at its face and finds the smile hasn't vanished. He starts to dig his nail into its thigh, peeling off flecks of red paint. When he sees that the clown hasn't changed its expression, he loses interest and looks at Sonny. Her gaze is fixed on a young girl in a school uniform eating an ice cream cone.

'Ash. This is the girl.'

'Who?'

'The schoolgirl who was recorded giving her boyfriend a blowjob on the school premises.'

'How do you know?'

'Just look at the strokes of her tongue. How she is swirling her tongue on the top and sucking the melted cream that is cascading down the sides of the cone. Ash. This is her!'

'Is that how a cock is sucked?' Ash asks, suppressing his excitement.

'Yes Ash. Madaan used to show me sick porn movies after we got married. He used to beg me to do all the things which those girls did. I refused. But I have seen enough of those movies to tell you that the girl who is having the ice cream is practising to blow her boyfriend.'

'What should we do Sonny?'

'Do you have a camera? We should take pictures.'

'No. I forgot to take it today.'

'Okay. Ash. I have an idea. But we will have to hurry up. The girl has already eaten half the ice cream.'

'Tell me.'

Sonny whispers something in Ash's ear.

The two wait patiently for the girl to come within hearing distance. They don't want to leave their seats as that would make them seem suspect. Sonny is focusing on the vanilla scoop that is now levelled. She fears that there might not be too much ice cream left for the girl to suck on it the way she was doing earlier. She has already started looking elsewhere when Ash slaps her on the thigh. She turns to see the girl standing close to them, facing away from her. She gives Ash the green signal.

The moment the girl touches the ice cream with the tip of her tongue, Ash starts moaning, 'Ah! Harder. Suck it harder.'

The girl looks around with a stunned expression, but only sees Sonny staring into the distance and Ash lying down with his head on the clown's lap.

She turns back and is about to lick the ice cream tentatively, when Ash shouts, 'I am cumming. I am about to cum!'

'Who is it?' she shouts. 'This is not funny. Really.' She looks around before saying, 'Ishaan, is that you?'

When she hears no response, she looks around again and finds an indifferent Sonny and Ash.

She tries to lick the ice cream again but can no longer get her tongue to touch it. She walks to the bin and throws the cone into it. Sonny and Ash wait for her to leave and start laughing.

'That was fun, Ash.'

'I know.'

'The bitch is going to think twice before giving anyone a blowjob.'

'But I still think that she was just an innocent, young girl.'

'No Ash. This world is full of evil people. You must not lose faith in what we do.'

'Okay, Sonny.'

The two are sitting inside the tea bar, Passionate Fruit, on the stools facing the self-service counter. Sonny chose it so that she could keep tabs on the customers' orders and, from them, gauge whether they have refined tastes and are well-off or not. There is a large drawing board at the back, where poems and letters written by young children have been pinned. Sonny catches a glimpse of the word 'scrumptious' written before 'iced tea' in one of the letters. She gets agitated and repeats the word out loud.

'Scrumteeyus. Scrumtuous.'

'Scrumshus,' Ash corrects her.

At first, Sonny doesn't react. But a few seconds later she starts shouting, 'That's the problem with these rich South Delhi parents. They employ tutors for their children when they are barely out of their wombs, and go out to parties and dos while their children are being put to sleep by South Indian or Nepali maids. I am sure that this word, however you pronounce it, has been written by one of the tutors. What do you say, Ash?'

'Doesn't seem so, Sonny. The writing looks like a child's,' Ash says, taking a closer look at the piece of paper troubling Sonny.

'Then the child's mother must be good at copying handwriting and must have written this down to impress other parents and customers.'

'Could be.'

'Not 'could be', Ash. Has to be! What you see on the surface is not true at all. Dig deeper and you'll find out why everything is so unjust and why we are suffering.'

Two customers, middle-aged men, arrive and order one masala tea each, in *kullars*. Sonny is sure that they are the nouveau rich from West Delhi who are spreading the plague of their bad taste among the posh South Delhi crowd. She doesn't like her rare sojourns to this part of Delhi to be disturbed by the backwardness of West Delhiites. She is sharpening her hate for the two men when she hears one of them talking on his phone, giving someone directions to his home. She can clearly hear him say Munirka, IIT flyover, Nehru Place – all locations in South Delhi. Not willing to accept that she was wrong, Sonny looks at his dishevelled hair, his paunch and casual footwear, and concludes that he is an unemployed man from West Delhi who is now living with his wife's parents in South Delhi. She gives him a disgusted look and complains to Ash that even her seven-year-old maid has the sense to order something more novel, especially when stepping outside the home and splurging at some restaurant.

'Uncultured people,' she snaps.

'Who?' Ash asks, looking at a handsome foreigner who is pounding away at the keyboard of his laptop.

'The two men who just took masala tea in the kullars.'

'Ah! Yes.'

'They should go to the New Delhi Railway Station and have tea there instead of coming to Passionate Fruit and spoiling our mood with their bad taste.'

'Yes, Sonny. I completely agree.'

The foreigner leaves his table and walks towards the counter after one of the waiters calls out his name. Sonny is looking at his order – some exotic flavoured tea with a dollop of cream on top and a pastry she doesn't recognise. She crosses her legs and starts smiling at him, hoping that he notices her and recognises her even when she is with Madaan in case their paths cross again. She can't wait to see the expression on her husband's face when such a refined man acknowledges her in public. She would love to see Madaan feel inferior in the man's presence and agree with what she has been trying to convey politely all these years – he is no match for her and their two sons have taken after their father. The foreigner gives her a passing glance but is more interested in his laptop. Ash's eyes are following his crotch, hidden behind the perfect fall of his black trousers. While Sonny is very impressed by the man and proud of the fact that she is sharing a space with him, Ash is hoping that he drops the drink on his trousers so the cloth clings to his body and lets him trace the outlines of his crotch. The two of them are busy observing the foreigner – Sonny, the way he picks up his fork and wipes the cream from his mouth; and Ash, the activity around his crotch when he shuffles his legs.

When the man has finished his meal and leaves the bar, Sonny and Ash come back to their senses and remember why they are there. Sonny takes out a tape recorder and plants it right at the centre of the table. She then ferrets through her pockets and fishes out two audio tapes from it. Both have white labels, one saying 'Sonny' and the other, 'Ash'.

'Don't you want anything to eat or drink?' Ash asks.

'After we've heard the tapes. Anyway which should we play first?' she asks.

'Play 'Ash.'

The tape gets stuck for the first few seconds, making a squeaky noise. Ash is worried that he might have failed to record the incident properly. He tries to grab hold of the tape, when a woman's scream bursts out of it. This is followed by a barrage of abuse hurled at a man whom she is calling a drunkard.

'That was my mother abusing my father when he started speaking about my grandfather's cancer.'

'Oh! Really, Ash?'

'Yes.'

'Now raise the volume. My father will say some interesting stuff.'

'The man made millions but didn't have the sense to get his prostate checked. He was coming over to Delhi to finalise his deals in pain but not once did he ask me if this pain was a symptom of something severe. Your entire family is like this. It doesn't think beyond money. Maybe that's why you keep taunting me because I haven't been able to earn much money.'

A couple seated right in front of them stares, but Sonny stares them down.

'Stop this at once,' a younger man's voice breaks in.

'That's my brother,' Ash says.

'Oh! You keep shut. Now, how much more money do you want us to spend on your next business project? Just tell me and I'll write you a cheque.'

'Stop it Papa. You're drunk.'

'You go upstairs, Jatan. See how Ash is doing. He takes all of this very badly. Let me handle this alcoholic man.'

'Alcoholic man with a healthy prostrate!'

'Please, Avnit. Please don't create a scene. It's my family's problem.'

'No. It's just that that your family likes taking your sister's husband's advice and not mine. Had I been told that he was in so much pain I would have brought him straight to Delhi and got all the tests done. Now you're coming to me crying that your father has cancer. All of you are the same.'

'You're just jealous because my father made a lot of money and you couldn't.'

There is the noise of glass shattering.

'You bitch! I am not jealous. I am just an unfortunate man who lost all his money when he married a woman from a family much poorer than his. Don't you get it? *You* are the cause of my downfall.'

'No, Avnit. Your drinking is. And you've been drinking since your college days.'

'I've been drinking because I have one son who is a failure, another who tried to kill himself, and a wife who just doesn't satisfy me.'

'Then leave me! Leave me and my sons alone.'

'I am planning to. I have already decided on buying a house in the hills and living a retired army officer's life.'

'Makes sense, Avnit, since you get most of your drinks from retired army officers.'

'I should have married my girlfriend from college. She is now a bigshot in Pune.'

'Yes. You should have Avnit. She was short, dark and ugly like you.'

'But at least she was a woman. Although even your sister Pranita is one hell of a woman.'

'How dare you talk about Pranita like this?'

'What a kisser! I still remember how she blew my mind during our trip to Cochin.'

'What do you mean?'

'I mean what I mean. Don't be naïve Rajni. You think your twenty-year-old sister tagged along with us to go boating with the kids or play monopoly with them? No! She was there for me! A man she knew her sister couldn't satisfy.'

'Stop this!'

Sonny stops the tape and looks at Ash.

'When was this?'

'A week ago. My grandfather was diagnosed with prostate cancer. Now it's in the last stages.'

'Should we continue playing this?' she asks him.

'No. Boring family secrets. Fast forward to the next recording. It's my brother making out in a car.'

'Oh! Ash. That's so creative of you.'

'Yes. I know.'

Sonny fast forwards the tape and stops when Ash asks her to.

They can hear moaning, the car seat creaking and the dashboard being struck. They hear something being unzipped and a plastic packet being torn.

Sonny tells Ash that his brother might be putting on a condom and the real fun might begin soon, but Ash cautions her by saying that he had seen the girl leave their home in a jacket and his brother might be trying to unzip it first. Sonny argues that the girl may have been reluctant to take off all her clothes as they were inside a car but Ash says that he knows his brother and that he doesn't like making out with girls with their clothes on. When she asks him how he knows, he tells her that he had once recorded him saying this to an ex-girlfriend. Sonny feels as if her world has come crashing down, but continues to hope that she can actually hear Ash's brother and the girl have sex. Ash sees the look on her face and consoles her by holding her hand.

For at least ten more minutes, Sonny and Ash are forced to make do with the latter's brother making out when, all of a sudden, there is the sound of the car horn blaring. Both of them jump off their seats and Ash starts laughing.

'My brother. He must have pressed the horn by mistake.'

'Oh! It scared the hell out of me.'

'It scared the hell out of me too.'

'Now listen.'

They hear someone banging on the door of the car. 'Hurry up. Put on your clothes.'

'Oh! Ash. The police! That's so funny!'

'I know.'

'Open the door,' a hoarse voice says.

'Just a second.'

'Open fast. This is the Delhi Police mobile patrol van.'

'Wait sir.'

The recording is disrupted for a while and when the sound returns, they hear Ash's brother telling the girl, 'Next time we'll try a hotel.'

'Try!' Sonny exclaims and starts laughing. 'Is he a virgin like you Ash?'

'Not any more, I think.'

'Why? Is there another recording where we can hear the two of them having sex?'

'No.'

'Okay. I liked your effort. Now, my turn.'

'Yes. Let's see what you have for me.'

Sonny plays her tape. The two of them hear nothing for the first thirty seconds except the noise of traffic and the chirping of birds. Ash begins to get annoyed, but soon they hear a ferocious growl.

'Ash. This is the stray bitch that lives outside House Number 14.'

'What is she doing?' he asks.

'She is trying to scare away a dog who is trying to mount her.'

'Really?'

'Yes.'

They hear the bitch growl again. This is followed by a slightly more masculine growl. Sonny tells Ash that this was when the bitch succumbed to the dog. There is silence for the next few minutes but for the dog's heavy breathing. Sonny says that she took the risk of standing right behind the fucking dogs for recording this.

Soon, they hear heavy taps followed by a man shouting abuses. Sonny says that a man was crossing House Number 14 with his family and started throwing stones at the two dogs so that his young daughter wouldn't have to witness the scene. They can hear the two dogs shriek, after which there is silence again.

Sonny raises the volume of the tape and, suddenly, the scream of a pup fills the bar.

All the customers start looking at their table. The manager steps out from behind the cash counter and starts walking towards Sonny and Ash.

'That was Jerry, Ash! My poor boy! He was standing right behind me when one of the pebbles hit him on his back.'

'Oh! Sonny. I am so sorry.'

'Excuse me. Can you please stop playing this in the bar?' the manager requests Sonny.

'Playing what?' Sonny asks irritably.

'This tape?'

'We are listening to the audio version of a movie. Do you have a problem?'

'No. But the customer sitting in front of you has complained that you are playing filthy stuff.'

'Alright. We'll leave. Ash, we'll do this someplace else, where people have the courtesy to mind their own business,' she shouts and the two of them leave Passionate Fruit.

They go to the pub, RGP. Young, middle-class boys and girls have queued up in front of the black counter behind which stand two strapping men – one taking the entry fee, the other tying a band round the couples' hands and giving them a chit. Sonny is sure that it contains directions to secret rooms in the pub where these depraved couples can make out. When she points out the man to Ash, he tries to calm her down by telling her that it is a coupon for free drinks.

'What drinks?'

'Two tequila shots.'

When the two reach the counter, the man taking the payment looks at Sonny carefully. She stares at him but the man continues to look at her and then at Ash.

'Are you sure you're together?'

'Yes. We are,' Ash says.

'Is that fine?' Sonny asks him in an angry tone.

'Sure.'

'How much?' Ash says.

'Four hundred for you. Free entry for the lady.'

Ash is about to reach for his wallet when Sonny grabs his hand.

'What?'

'I am going to pay.'

'Why Sonny?'

'Because this was my plan.'

'But...'

'Please. Let's just go inside.'

When the other man tries to tie the band on Sonny, she snatches it from him.

'You are not my sister,' she shouts at him.

'What Madam?'

'I'll wear it myself.'

'Alright, Madam. Calm down.'

The two find a corner seat so they can clearly see all the couples. There is a cylindrical lampshade on the top and the tables are separated by a small wrought iron grill. A waiter hands them a menu card that has a list of drinks on the front and salads and appetizers on the back. Sonny doesn't bother to read it and passes it on to Ash, who tosses it aside.

The bar has two rows of bottles and the wall behind them is changing colour: blue to green and green to blue. Green lasers are scything through the front of the bar counter, to the back of the rows of drinks, all the way to the top of the wall. The DJ is playing right next to the bar; his table littered with empty CD cases and song requests written down on snippets of paper in drunken scrawls. Right now, the dance floor is almost empty and the only ones in the spirit of dancing seem to be the restless waiters and bartenders who sometimes, briefly, show off a move while climbing up the stairs or pouring drinks.

Sonny and Ash wait patiently for the dance floor to fill up. When, after half an hour, they see just two couples dancing, Sonny blames it on the DJ's poor choice of music. When she remembers Madaan telling her that being a DJ was very fashionable these days and also lucrative, she starts hating her sons Gaurav and

Vinod for opting for medicine and human resource management respectively and not becoming DJs. She also plans on fighting with her husband tonight for making Gaurav take up medicine to make sure there was at least one doctor in the family to carry on his father's legacy. She might as well have spent money on getting her tummy fat removed, instead of buying a synthesiser and drums for Gaurav for his school band. When she complains to Ash about the bad music, he tells her that it is a weekday and that he has heard the dance floor fills up only after 3 pm. The two almost fall asleep on the table, when a young man taps Ash on the shoulder.

'Hi! Could you please make room for my wife?'

Sonny instantly looks up to see a woman in an advanced stage of pregnancy. She looks at Ash and the two play footsie under the table in excitement.

They shift to the edge of their seat and the woman cautiously takes a step inside and sits down. The man whispers something in her ear, gently caresses her stomach and disappears into the synthetic darkness of the pub. Both Sonny and Ash feel awkward as they can neither talk nor look at the dance floor.

The pregnant woman lip syncs for a while before turning to the two of them and saying, 'I am Nandita. You?'

'I am Sonny. This is Ash,' Sonny says casually.

'Quite odd for a couple. Family, I guess.'

Ash grabs hold of Sonny's hand and presses it so that she doesn't lose her temper.

'Not a couple. Becoming closer than a family,' Sonny manages to say.

'Wow! Isn't this world beautiful? So full of possibilities... Look at me. I was never keen to have a child but once I met Rahul

I couldn't imagine a life without something that the two of us shared so intimately.'

'How wonderful,' Sonny exclaims.

'So what made you come here?' Ash asks.

'Actually, we had no plans to come to a pub – certainly not during the afternoon and with my advanced pregnancy, but Rahul said he wanted to celebrate the baby's arrival. We are here to have lunch and look for a book of baby names. Rahul is stuck on Anindita while I think Arundhati is the best name for a girl.'

'How do you know it's a girl?' Sonny asks, rising from the seat.

'Just wishful thinking. I have three brothers and Rahul has one younger brother. Our families are full of men. So we're just hoping that the baby who comes into our life balances the family sex ratio.'

'Delusional bitch,' Sonny mutters and Ash yells to drown her comment.

'What happened, Ash?'

'That's my favourite song. I kind of like cheering the singers.'

'Yes. *Bittersweet Symphony* is just amazing,' Nandita says.

'So, aren't the two of you going to dance?' she asks Sonny and Ash.

'No. We are not desperate you see. We can wait for the dance floor to fill up,' Sonny snaps.

'It's not about being desperate. It's about losing yourself to such a liberating physical expression.'

Sonny is about to say something when the man returns with a drink. He leaves it on the table and carries away Nandita in his arms as she screams in joy. The two of them are one of the first couples on the dance floor.

At around 3.30 pm, the dance floor is filled with young couples. The enthusiasm is so high that one couple is dancing on the seats and another on the steps leading to the smoking area and the entrance. The whole pub is throbbing with music.

Sonny and Ash leave their tables, hold hands and make their way to the floor. They find a sliver of space between two couples – two latecomers and Nandita and her husband who are right next to the DJ. Sonny plugs her right ear with her index finger and hopes that she doesn't get a migraine, while Ash tries to feel up the crotches and sweaty armpits of men. Nandita smiles at Sonny and tries to make some space for her by putting her arms around her husband and holding him tight. He is gently tapping his fingers on her stomach, at times bending down to kiss it and press his ear against it.

Sonny smiles stiffly and steps into the space holding Ash with one hand. The two dance tentatively to heavy trance music, Sonny doing little more than swaying her hips and Ash clenching his fists and moving them in an arc.

Suddenly, a fight breaks out in the middle of the dance floor and those on the fringes are pushed back further. Two drunken girls, both dressed in black, are fighting with one another.

'I'll fuck your Mom, you whore!' one shouts.

'You see for yourself – I'll fuck *your* Mom.'

'Girls like you are available at every corner to fuck men!' the other retaliates.

The first girl takes out her cell phone and starts dialling a number shouting, 'She's gone – this is her last day!'

Before she can start talking, the girls' boyfriends leap at one another and start beating each other up. Two bouncers arrive to clear the dance floor and the couples start running towards the stairs.

Sensing a chance, Sonny nudges Ash and whispers, 'Do it Ash! Come on! What has the world given us?'

Ash hesitates for a bit before clenching his fist and punching Nandita hard in the stomach.

A scream rings out and everyone turns their heads. Nandita drops down on her knees, breathing through her mouth. She looks down to see spots of blood on her skirt. She screams, holding her stomach, and falls sideways, her head hitting the wooden floor. Her husband grabs hold of the man standing next to him and starts beating him. The man's girlfriend tries to stop him by saying that her boyfriend had nothing to do with what happened but he is in no mood to listen.

Both Sonny and Ash stealthily make their way across the dance floor and leave RPG.

'Ash! That was brave.'

'I feel bad Sonny. Do you think I killed the baby?'

'Maybe. Maybe not. But don't you think it would have been worse if he had been born and turned out like my two sons?'

'There's that, too.'

Chapter 5

It is early in the afternoon and Sonny is sprawled on a chaise lounge, almost kissing the parapet of her rooftop. She is clad in a tight-fitting pink swimming costume that reveals clusters of fat. She is sipping a green drink with a straw and splashing her feet in a tub of water. Ash is seated next to her with his back upright and not wearing the trunks Sonny had requested him to. He has also quietly picked up his small tub of water and placed it next to the servant quarters. A glass of the green drink is lying next to his chaise lounge. Sonny keeps motioning at Ash to drink it but he hasn't touched it again after taking a sip.

When Sonny requested Ash to come over to her house during their morning walk, he thought that she might want him to work on Jerry's 'Missing' posters again. Instead, he was shocked to see her clad in a swimming costume with a towel wrapped around her waist, asking him to come up to the rooftop. There, Ash found sand scattered all over and artificial crab shells placed over it. Two chaise lounges stood with two tubs full of water right below them. When he gave Sonny a quizzical look, she handed him an oversized, slightly crushed pair of brown swimming trunks. She told him that it belonged to her elder son, Gaurav, and that she wanted him to wear it. Ash controlled his urge to immediately grab it and sniff at the portion where Gaurav's testicles must have lain, and slapped himself hard on his right thigh. Sonny stared at him and told him to treat himself better. He told her that it was alright and that he was used to the pain. She walked up to him and pressed the tip of her finger in his thigh. He flinched. She warned him not to lie to her again. He apologised and asked her the plan for the day.

'We are in Mauritius today, Ash,' she exclaimed, unable to contain her delight.

'Why? Why now? And why Mauritius?'

'Oh, Ash! It's the tenth anniversary of our trip to Mauritius that never happened. I always celebrate it. It's the only secret I have that Madaan knows and tolerates. Of course, if he comes to know about what we talk about and do, he would leave me. But he allows me to do this since he, too, feels the brunt of missing out on that trip.'

'Why would cancelling a trip abroad matter, Sonny?'

Sonny took Ash by the hand and guided him to the chaise lounge. She made sure he was comfortable, handed him his glass, turned her own chaise lounge in his direction and sat down. Holding her drink, she told him how, on this same day ten years ago, her life changed.

While she was packing her luggage for their week-long Mauritius trip – their first trip outside India – and Madaan was taking a bath, her mother-in-law collapsed on the floor of her bedroom. Worried that Madaan might make a last-minute cancellation, she locked the bathroom door from the outside and ran to her room. She held her mother-in-law up and helped her to a chair. She then shook her with all her might, slapping her and accusing her of trying to sabotage their trip. All she got in reply was incoherent sputtering as her mother-in-law held her hand to her heart. Sonny splashed a jug of water on her face. Madaan had started shouting and pulling at the door. Sonny knew that the trip was cancelled and that her mother-in-law – mostly by cruel intent – had succeeded in destroying her social ambitions. Wearing a defeated look, she walked out and opened the bathroom door for Madaan to come to his ailing mother's aid.

There was one more reason why Sonny had wanted them to make the trip come what may – the fact that Madaan had taken a loan, upon her insistence, to fund their trip. Now the money would be squandered on saving an old woman's life and Sonny would have to put up with the vivid holiday accounts of her friends who were better off than her – something that irked Madaan as well.

'Ash, I can write a thesis on our ex-friends' holiday accounts. They were so detailed. And we were not even in a position to cut ties with them since both our sons were friends with their children.'

'So, what did you do about it?'

Sonny told him that she had spent many sleepless nights to come up with a plan to break her relationship with one of the couples, as the other one had not been holidaying since the woman's father's death. One night, over dinner, she had even suggested this to Madaan but he had said that the next time they talked about their gambling trips in Kathmandu, or their skiing trips in the Alps, he'd simply tell them that he had already read all about them in travel guides and would like to discuss something else. Sonny found his idea workable but not entirely convincing.

After all, if any of her friends had the slightest inkling that these details were bothering Sonny and Madaan, then it would be considered a major social victory. So Sonny decided to take the matter in her own hands and use her younger son Vinod's friendship with the couple's daughters to fulfill her plan. She didn't mind if Vinod was blamed if things turned out the way she desperately wanted them to.

'Why? Why Vinod?' Ash asked, with one eye on the crushed pair of swimming trunks lying on Sonny's lap.

Sonny could never forgive her younger son Vinod. How could she? She had conceived him while preparing for her second year MBA exams. The bastard was so demanding even as a foetus that Sonny suffered from perpetual nausea and abdominal pain and had to give up on her studies midway. She had convinced herself that she would resume her studies after the child was born, and dump it in the care of her mother-in-law (who was healthy and active then). But, barely a couple of months after his birth, her mother-in-law fell sick and Sonny had to leave her studies indefinitely. There was another reason why her second pregnancy and Vinod's birth brought her so much discomfort – Sonny was never able to shed the twenty kilos she had gained. Sometimes, when she looked at Vinod or talked to him over the phone, she couldn't help looking down at her flabby stomach and squeeze the fat in pure hatred for the boy.

'What was the plan?' he asked her.

'Ash. I was helpless. But I had to do something because I couldn't bear hearing another word about the couple's foreign trips. Not after our trip was cancelled. Moreover, the couple I was targeting had already left for their one month vacation in the US and I had very little time to plan things.'

'What did you do? Tell me,' he said, shifting in his seat.

'Ash. I failed, probably because I didn't have a partner like you.'

'Tell me, Sonny. It's alright. I won't tell anyone.'

'Promise me, Ash,' she said, wiping away a tear.

'I promise.'

Sonny needed to find out the details of their trip and she was sure Vinod would know. So, one day, she decided to surprise Vinod and invite him out to Nirula's for a pizza. The ten-year-old boy was taken aback since she had never taken him anywhere alone, although she and Gaurav went out together frequently. Over their meal, Sonny wiggled the details of the trip out of him. Her only hope, she realised, rested on Disneyland.

'Disneyland?'

'Yes, Ash.'

'How?'

'Vinod used to exchange letters with the couple's twin daughters and had promised to write them a letter while they were holidaying in the States. My only chance lay with Disneyland because the girls were adamant about going. But one of them suffered from severe motion sickness. So, Vinod had said during lunch, the father had decided not to go there to keep her from feeling left out.'

Sonny immediately realised that if Vinod could write to the girls saying they should definitely visit Disneyland or all their friends would make fun of them, she could create a situation in which the daughter who suffered from motion sickness would actually go for a ride and fall sick. Sonny persuaded her son to write this in his letter and spent the next month praying that the girls would fall sick or be involved in some freak accident.

'Did the plan work out?'

'No, Ash. The girls went on all the daring rides. The one who had motion sickness didn't even feel anything! I think there is something special about America's air. It rejuvenates you. And look at us – suffering in this hopeless, stinking country of ours.'

The seven-year-old maid ushers in a fat woman with greying hair and a sagging stomach. The little girl is wearing a tattered blue dress and walking with a limp. She stops after a couple of steps, bends down and holds her right knee. Ash sees her pitiful condition and is about to get up from his chair to help her when Sonny stops him.

'Leave her alone. I am doing her a favour by keeping her. She can't cook, can't wash clothes and can barely clean the utensils. All she does well is feed my mother-in-law two meals a day.'

'What's her name?' Ash asks her.

'She can't even speak, Ash, so I have decided to call her 'girl'. All I know is that she was on her way to Delhi with her parents from her village in Jharkhand, when their train collided with two elephants while crossing a wildlife sanctuary and got derailed. Her parents suffered head injuries and died. In a cruel twist of fate, this bitch survived and was brought to Delhi for work by one of her uncles who had kept her under his roof for six months. But he couldn't fend for her any longer.

I found her through a recruitment agency in Vasant Kunj. When I went there to interview her, the man lied to me, saying that she wasn't speaking because she had contracted a throat infection. He also said that the *elaichi* tea I was drinking had been prepared by her. He even told me that she was eighteen years old and looked like a child because of her stunted growth. I desperately needed domestic help, so I ended up giving the agent an advance annual commission for an adult helper. His only request to me was to give her at least two full meals a day and not to make her sleep in the bathroom. I wanted to tell the bastard that I was doing him a favour by hiring her. But I agreed, telling him that I had a spacious servant quarter on the rooftop for the girl. Actually, that room had just about enough space for a litter of kittens. Usually, these agents do a recce of the house and living conditions of the owner. I showed him an image of the small storeroom at Madaan Chemists on my cellphone. He asked me about the piles of boxes with medicines in them. I told him that the boxes contained the new furniture we had purchased for our maid. He was pleasantly surprised but when I sensed he might ask for a recce I went up to the girl and squeezed her cheeks saying, after all a girl is a Lakshmi who brings wealth and joy to a family. The man immediately handed her over to me.

For the first few weeks, I didn't find anything suspicious about the girl. But when she started behaving like a child – crying without any reason, making strange faces, playing with the miniatures while cleaning the living room – I decided to expose the agent's lie. That is when I bought her a pair of panties and made her wear them. I told her to leave her used panties in a small basket outside her quarters every morning. When I didn't see any blood on it for a month, I went to the agent again to fire him. He revealed that she was just seven years old and had no one to look after her. I was relieved because I was able to bring down the annual commission by fifty percent.

It's taken me three months to train her and still she is mostly useless. Now, her uncle from Jharkhand wants her back but she refuses to go because he probably wants to fuck her.'

The maid leaves the woman with Sonny and Ash and promptly disappears. The woman greets Sonny with a smile and squats right next to her. She pulls her sari down to her ankles and covers her head with her pallu. She eyes Ash inquisitively.

'Gauri, this is Ash. The boy I told you about,' Sonny says.

'Okay, Madam.'

'Ash, this is Gauri. She tells me everything going on in the colony. Such an angel she is,' Sonny exclaims, fidgeting on the chaise lounge. 'Oh, Gauri! How much I love you!' Sonny gets up from her chair and pulls the maid's fat cheeks. Gauri smiles and looks down at the floor, embarrassed.

Sonny leans back in her chair and says, 'Now tell me Gauri. What information do you have for me?'

'Lots, Madam!' Gauri replies, shielding her forehead from the sun.

'Tell us then. What's stopping you?'

'House Number 3's Mishra got into a fight with young army jawans outside the army mess. He was bashed up so badly that he is now nursing a broken rib and a fracture in a hospital.'

'Really?' Sonny asks excitedly.

'Yes, Madam.'

'What happened?'

'You must be aware of Mishra's mental illness. The poor man went into deep depression after he lost his younger son in a car accident. He had, very recently, started recovering after joining a meditation course at some foundation. He used to meditate early in the morning and at night, after dinner. But you know, Madam, how difficult it is for this colony to sleep when it has a mess facing it and corrupt officers renting out space for the marriage of civilians. So, two days ago, during a marriage ceremony, Mishra couldn't focus on his mediation because of the music blaring out of the loudspeakers. He decided to walk down to the mess and confront the guards. He carried his cell phone along and even threatened the guard that he would dial 100 if they didn't stop the celebrations immediately. That night, the daughter of a senior army officer's civilian friend was getting married and, when Mishra decided to break the barricade at the entrance, the guards started beating him up. The police have not made any arrests as the army is saying that they'll try the jawans in their courts.

These army people think that they can get away with murder. I hope we have a war soon so that they are on the border fighting enemies and taking bullets rather than taking cuts from civilians to organise weddings.'

'Really?' Ash asks.

'Of course, Ash. It's an open secret. No one is more hypocritical than them. They have blocked Mall Road, Polo Road and Parade Road for civilians and for 'the safety of sensitive areas' but, when they have a marriage ceremony, then all these roads are opened.'

'But how can civilians hold functions at an army mess?'

'It's easy, Ash. They book the hall in an officer's name saying that they are related to him.'

'Oh!'

'Anyway, go on Gauri dear. Tell me more.'

'Madam, you know House number 15's Mr Narain?'

'Yes, Gauri. He used to bring his daughter to the chemist store to pick up ointment for their dog's skin allergy.'

Gauri laughs so hard that she almost keels over.

'Tell me, Gauri. What's so funny?'

'Madam, the ointment was for the daughter, not for the dog. Mrs Narain had told her husband to tell the chemist that it was for the dog because she didn't want her daughter's value to go down in the marriage market. Everyone knows that she is thirty and had an affair for two years.'

'Where exactly does she have the skin problem?' Sonny asks, looking at Ash who smiles at her.

'On her legs.'

'Oh!' Sonny says with an air of disappointment.

'Don't worry, Madam. It's causing them a lot of problems.'

'How?'

'Their father is looking for a groom for her, but all of them first want to see her in a skirt.'

Both Sonny and Ash start laughing hysterically.

'Really?' Sonny finally manages to ask. 'Did the prospective grooms really say that?'

'Yes, Madam.'

'So what did Mr Narain tell them?'

'Nothing, Madam. He simply had to back out.'

'But doesn't Mr Narain have an elder daughter too?'

'Yes, he does. She is thirty two and still unmarried.'

'Why?' both Sonny and Ash ask in unison.

'Actually, Madam, she likes a man who is in love with her – or that's what I am told. But the man's parents want the wedding to take place at a five star hotel.'

'So?'

'Mr Narain! He runs a guest house in South Delhi where many high profile marriages take place. He has refused to arrange the ceremonies in a five star hotel because he feels that they would be a needless expense. Also, it would be an insult to his guest house. The parents are fighting over the time for the dinner. The boy's family prefer an early dinner while Mr Narain plans to set it up at 11 pm.'

'Why at 11 pm?' Sonny asks.

'Madam, it's a new tactic employed by girls' families to save money. It's simple – many guests leave by 11 pm and the cost of the dinner goes down.'

'Oh, how innovative!' Sonny is impressed.

'I agree,' Ash says.

'What then, Gauri?'

'Nothing, Madam. Both the girl and the boy have been hanging on to one another while their parents are fighting over the venue. But the boy's father is adamant. He said that he got his daughter married in a five star hotel and wants the same treatment, now that it's his turn to benefit from having a son. This has been going on for over a year. The boy runs his father's business and doesn't have the financial independence to live with the girl on his own, even though she is ready to leave her father's house.'

'Tit for tat,' Ash says.

'I know Ash. What a cruel world, isn't it? Anyway, Gauri, what happened to House Number 10's son? Is he still being tutored at home?'

'No, Madam. He has been packed off to a boarding school. Just one week after going there, he started sending letters to his parents threatening to commit suicide if they didn't take him back.'

'So, what have the parents done?'

'Nothing. They sold off some property they owned in DLF and bought a house in Dehradun. It's close to the hostel and the mother stays there now so she can visit her son all the time.'

'So the boy is responsible for separating his parents?'

'Yes, Madam. They had no choice.'

Sonny fantasises about the woman spending lonely nights in Dehradun and craving for her husband's body. Ash thinks about the husband. He has seen the man and thought that he looked like a person who may be interested in young boys. He imagines the man doing to him everything he had been doing to his wife. But when he remembers his bristly white moustache, the hair creeping out of his ears, and the black mole on his left cheek, he retches.

Sonny goes up to Ash and starts rubbing his back.

'What's wrong dear? Do you want Gauri to come some other time?'

'No. It's okay. I think the drink didn't suit me.'

'Don't worry, Ash. I didn't lace yours with liquor. Mine has some gin in it, though.'

'Really?'

'Yes. I allow myself some alcohol on holidays, and today we are in Mauritius.'

'What, Madam?' Gauri asks.

'Nothing dear. Now you can go. I'll pay you for today and next week together. And please get me some information about Mr Goel's daughter. The last time you told me that his daughter was having problems conceiving. You never told me what happened after that.'

'Madam, I don't work for them any more. But I'll ask Shanti.'

'No. Don't even talk about Shanti. She stole my jewellery while she was working for me – that's why I had to throw her out.'

'Really, Madam?'

'Yes.'

'But I thought Shanti became very subdued after that unfortunate incident.'

'No, Gauri. Now you can leave.'

Ash has dozed off while Sonny is refilling her glass with the green drink from a jug. She takes small sips from it and lies splayed on the chaise lounge, soaking in the wet Mauritian summer. After she has finished the drink, she walks down to the sand and wallows in it, hoping that Ash joins her there. Soon, she hears her maid trying to force feed her mother-in-law. She had seen the spectacle once and was totally repulsed. The maid had stood on a round wooden stool whose legs had been pared down by the carpenter so that she didn't have to bend too much. She then held the old woman from behind till she had found a comfortable perch. She had forced spoonfuls of porridge into her mouth. The old lady took in very little and coughed out the rest, leaving blotches and trails on her shrunken face and neck. The maid would wipe herself and pick up the pieces of regurgitated food with tissue paper and throw them in the dustbin, but Sonny had warned her not to waste even a morsel. Now, the little girl simply pressed the hollow of the spoon against the old woman's mouth so that she was unable to open it, and even if she did, the mush would stick to the spoon.

Once her mother-in-law stops her low pitched squealing – her way of protesting against the force feeding – Sonny decides to take a nap, facing Ash. Suddenly she recalls Madaan's complaint to her in the morning. He had said he could smell shit in his mother's room, while he checked her pulse. Sonny had pacified him with a lie about the girl having an upset stomach and not being able to control her bowels, when the truth was that she hadn't changed the old woman's diapers for a whole day.

Her mother-in-law's diapers also had a story behind them.

When Sonny was without a maid and had to clean her mother-in-law and change her into new clothes, she carried out the task meticulously, for fear of falling sick from the persistent faecal odour. Even after the girl had come to stay, Sonny continued to change the diapers whenever she dirtied them. During this ordeal, she turned to the television for relief. Sonny would watch cookery shows in Hindi so that she lost her appetite for the next meal and was able to shed the weight she had put on because of that bastard Vinod. While her mother-in-law writhed on her old, teak chair Sonny would often whisper into her ear: 'This is the only benefit of cleaning your shit, you mad, old woman.' She would not say a word and look at her daughter-in-law with stony eyes. After Bela had sent an SMS to her elder brother about how her mother was uttering the word 'London' and needed to go there, Sonny made sure that she didn't watch any English channels in case the word 'London' was uttered and the mad woman started repeating it again.

One day, her sister-in-law, Bela had dropped in to see her mother. She was very polite to Sonny, but when she went back home she sent an SMS to her elder brother and made a call to Madaan to complain that Sonny didn't clean her mother properly and that she smelt of shit. Sonny was enraged as she had changed the old woman's diaper, sponged her body with Dettol and dusted Johnson's baby powder on her bottom only a few hours ago. When Madaan confronted her after having been scolded by his rich brother in the UK, she laughed, saying that his sister and her family's shit must smell of Dettol and Johnson's baby powder.

Madaan didn't take the complaint lightly, though, and decided to stay home for two days to oversee Sonny changing diapers and point out her flaws. He made life miserable for her by his mere presence. That is when Sonny came up with a plan. For days, she feigned depression and coaxed Madaan into getting a pup so that she could leave him in the house and he could shit wherever he wanted. This was the only way she could divert Madaan's attention from the smell of his mother's shit. For the entire two months that Jerry stayed in their house, he had left his smelly droppings all over, and both she and Madaan had to clean up after him. During this period, Sonny stopped cleaning her mother-in-law regularly to get back at her sister-in-law. When her sister-in-law smelled shit on her mother once again and complained to Madaan, he said that it must be Jerry's. Sonny overheard the conversation and was delighted by her plan's success. Sadly, just two weeks later, Jerry had vanished, leaving her with no option but to start the cleaning ritual again.

'Jerry!' Sonny screams, almost falling off the chaise lounge.

Ash wakes up fearing that something might have happened to his partner in crime.

'What happened, Sonny? Why are you remembering Jerry all of a sudden?'

'Oh, Ash! It's a very long story. I'll tell you some other time. Right now I am in the mood to have some fun.'

'What kind of fun?'

'The kind of fun the two of us have.'

'Do you have any ideas up your sleeve?'

'Yes. And a bright one, I must say.'

'Let's get on with it.'

'Really, Ash? Why are you so good to me? It's strange really, since the whole world is cruel to me. I wish there were more men like you around.'

'Thanks, Sonny.'

Sonny and Ash are sitting cross-legged in the sand. Sonny is searching for numbers in a small, black diary while Ash is looking at her anxiously.

'Did you find the numbers?'

'Yes, Ash. But maybe these men are back from their reconnaissance mission. Gauri gave these numbers to me a long time back. Who knows, some officers might have been transferred by now, or might have even left the army.'

'How many numbers do you have?' Ash asks, twiddling his thumbs.

'Five.'

'That means five prospective victims.'

'Yes, Ash.'

'I don't see any harm in trying.'

'Alright.'

Nobody responds at the first two numbers. When Sonny is about to dial the third number, Ash tells her to try the first two numbers again. No response. Sonny wonders if Gauri gave her the wrong numbers but she doubts it since the veteran maid of the colony has never given her wrong information before. She tries the third number. The phone rings for more than thirty seconds and, just when Sonny is about to hang up, she hears a woman's throaty voice.

Sonny gets so excited that she drops the cordless phone, but Ash manages to catch it before it falls.

'Talk, Ash! We're third time lucky,' Sonny whispers, tugging at his collar.

Ash clears his throat and starts speaking.

'Commanding Officer Monga this side. Can I speak to Captain Batra's wife?'

'Speaking.'

'I am sorry to inform you Ma'am that your husband lost his life in a reconnaissance mission near his posting.'

There is silence for a while. Ash smirks at Sonny, and both wait for Captain Batra's wife to say something, when they hear a man's voice.

'Hi. Captain Batra here.'

Ash immediately disconnects the call and holds the receiver against his chest.

'What happened?'

'I just heard Captain Batra's voice.'

'Oh! So we failed. That's okay.'

'Let's try the fourth number. Maybe we'll be fourth time lucky.'

Sonny dials the fourth number. This time, someone answers almost instantly. A fresh, sweet voice. Sonny throws the phone at Ash. He catches it and clears his throat.

'Commanding officer Krishna here. Can I speak to Captain Khanna's wife?'

'Speaking.'

'I am afraid your husband lost his life in a reconnaissance mission near his posting.'

Again, there is silence for a while. Then the woman breaks down. Ash switches to speaker phone mode.

'How did he die? Did he leave any message for me? I had a bad feeling about his operation. Please tell me. Please.'

Both Sonny and Ash giggle as the woman continues to plead.

'I am sorry. The body will be flown down to Delhi tomorrow morning. Your husband was a brave man and died fighting his country's enemies. I salute him.'

'I know. It was always his passion to join the army. But who is going to look after my two-year-old son and the baby I am pregnant with?' the woman asks, sobbing.

'Don't worry. You'll find a way. It was my duty to inform you about this terrible incident. Goodbye.'

Sonny and Ash roll with laughter. When they stand up they are covered in sand. The two of them take turns wiping it off their bodies, sometimes throwing it back in each other's faces.

Chapter 6

Sonny and Ash turn into a narrow, crammed lane in one of Hauz Khas's residential areas. She had asked the cab driver to drop them at the local market so that they could walk down to the astrology centre and compensate for the morning walk they would be missing. Sonny is dressed in an oversized sweatshirt and black pyjamas, while Ash is wearing a shirt and trousers. Although he was hesitant to dress formally, Sonny had convinced Ash to dress up so that the astrologer judged him solely on the basis of the position of the planets in his chart and not his looks. When Ash told her that he was not interested in knowing his future, she said that he could at least give her company while she asked the astrologer questions that were worrying her.

Sonny is also wearing a red pouch around her waist that is full of objects that jangle every time she takes a step. She stops from time to time, feeling the pouch to assure herself. Ash is busy looking out for a board that says 'Future Zone'. They reach the end of the lane and rest their tired bodies against the back of a car.

When Ash sees Sonny feeling the objects again he asks her, 'What are these?'

'My private possessions, Ash!'

'Can I have a look?'

'Sure!'

Sonny unzips the pouch and takes out a cordless phone, a television remote control, a small clock and a hundred rupee note with reddish brown stains on it.

'You're carrying your home with you Sonny!' Ash smiles.

'I had to Ash. I had no other option.'

'Why? What happened?'

Sonny tells Ash that she had an argument with Madaan just before they left for Hauz Khas.

'In the morning, when he had gone to check on his mother, he found that the toilet seat in her bathroom had cracked. Bela and her twenty-year-old son Raghav were coming over to meet my mother-in-law, and he didn't want them to injure themselves using the toilet. He decided to keep our bedroom door open so that they had access to our bathroom. I told Madaan categorically that I would not allow my sister-in-law to cast her evil eye on my bedroom. The two of them could lift the toilet seat and go. When Madaan argued that it would be inconvenient for them, I reminded him of their old, West Patel Nagar flat where there were three Indian-style bathrooms. Had his parents sent their children to relieve themselves in their rich neighbour's Western style bathrooms?

Madaan was quiet for a few seconds before revealing the real reason – Raghav was going to settle down in the States and Madaan could use him to send foreign drugs in bulk, which he could later sell in the black market.

Realising that my husband's decision could improve our financial prospects, even though it was a case of too little too late,

I agreed to keep the bedroom door open, provided I could take all my precious belongings with me. Madaan agreed, probably thinking that I would lock them in the almirah where I lock up the snacks.'

'That's very wise of you Sonny,' Ash says. 'But what about that hundred rupee note?'

'Oh, Ash! That was the money I had offered to the goddess after going to the temple. I left her small figurine there, but brought back the hundred rupee note.'

Ash sniggers.

'Ash, I told the goddess that I had no other option but to take the hundred rupee note and that I'd bring it back as soon as my sister-in-law and her son left. I am sure she understands.'

'I hope so, Sonny.'

The two of them are leaning against the car, Sonny resting her head on Ash's shoulder. He has one eye on Sonny's belongings scattered at the back of the car, and the other looking out for anyone walking in their direction so that he can stop them and ask about Future Zone. When he doesn't see anyone for a while, he shuts his eyes and falls asleep.

Ash is jolted awake by loud conversation in a language he doesn't know. He gets up with a shudder and looks to his right to see a South Indian couple standing outside a small gate. The two of them are poring over a red file. The man is feverishly flipping through its crisp white pages. The woman is moving her finger along the page, as the man mumbles rapidly under his breath. The two continue to do this for a while, before a dark-complexioned, plump girl who resembles the woman, walks out of the gate and joins them. She is wearing thick-rimmed spectacles and her hair is pulled back in two stiff pig tails. Her white skirt reaches till her ankles and, as it billows in the breeze, reveals a trail of hair on her legs.

Ash gets excited and shakes Sonny who wakes up with a shriek and quickly puts her belongings back into the pouch.

'Sonny, that South Indian couple just came out of Future Zone.'

'Let me see, Ash.'

Sonny observes the couple for a few seconds and starts smiling.

'Ash, they are here because of the girl's dark skin.'

'Really?'

'Of course, Ash! She looks quite old to me. Must be in her mid-thirties. Unable to find a match because of her dark complexion.'

'No, Sonny. My brother has dated two girls who were darker than him.'

'But not as ugly as this girl, Ash?'

'That's true, Sonny. Not as ugly.'

'Exactly. Anyway, the good thing is that now we won't have to go looking for Future Zone. Also, I hope you are carrying the towel and the bottle I gave you?'

'I am, Sonny.'

'Good. Let's go now.'

On their way to the entrance of Future Zone, Sonny tells Ash how Bela's son Raghav is already engaged to a rich exporter's daughter. When Ash expresses his surprise saying that the boy is too young to tie the knot, she nods in agreement.

'I was surprised too. My maid was sick that morning so, when Bela called, I had to go to my mother-in-law's room and hold the cordless telephone against her ears. Bela has this bad habit of keeping her dying mother updated on every bit of news, even though the latter hasn't responded even once. She said that even though her mother was not with her physically, she was sure that, subconsciously, she understood everything. I had already told Madaan that I was not going to be a part of this futile exercise and had shown the girl how to hold the phone against my mother-in-law's ears and what button to press to disconnect the call.

That morning, Bela had called up to inform her mother that Raghav had landed a lucrative job in a New York multinational. I heard Bela's delight at the fact that Raghav was financially independent at such a young age, even though her husband wanted him to join the ancestral business as he was their only son. Bela thanked her mother for marrying her off to such a wealthy man and tearfully remembered her father, because of whose exemplary deeds as a doctor their family's financial condition had been overlooked by her late father-in-law. She told her mother how Raghav had also been able to find an apartment in Manhattan and was ready to take on this new life.

However, the extensive travelling that the job entailed was giving Bela sleepless nights. Raghav would have to travel to Amsterdam and Bangkok among other places, and Bela was afraid that he might visit prostitutes and contract AIDS. So, she had spoken to her husband and decided to get Raghav engaged to a girl from a respectable family so that he wouldn't have to look around whenever he couldn't control his sexual urges. I couldn't control my laughter and Bela disconnected, fearing that someone might have overheard her.

I didn't hear anything about Raghav's marriage plans all week and Bela didn't call up even once. Then, one night, Madaan came home all excited and hugged me. When I asked him why he was so overjoyed, he told me that Bela had found a suitable match for Raghav. When I reminded him that his sister was one of the reasons behind our constant financial hardships, he whispered gently in my ears that the girl's family had a history of cancer – her grandfather, two uncles, one aunt and younger brother had all died after prolonged battles with the disease. Madaan knew their family physician and he had informed him that her father had just undergone tests for a cyst and that he was sure that it was malignant. Since Madaan was Raghav's uncle, the man would feel compelled to buy all the medicines from their store. After two long years, we'd get a permanent source of income from one patient. He added that the man was also very well connected and could send more customers his way. I wasn't impressed with his projections at all, but pretended that I was so that he could tell me more about the girl and why Bela hadn't called her mother up to inform her of such a major development.

Madaan told me that Bela wanted a girl with a fair complexion and whose family didn't have any issues if she travelled with her fiancé before marriage. Since no respectable family would allow their daughter to do so, Bela had started looking for slightly older girls who had been married before. He told me that he understood Bela's obsession with fair skin, since she was married to a dark man, but he didn't understand why she had imposed the condition of travelling before marriage. Finally, she was able to find a girl who was older than Raghav by five years and had been married once before. Bela went to her house in Rajouri Garden, saw that the girl was fair and talked to her privately. When the girl agreed to all the conditions and Raghav liked the girl too, Bela announced that the two of them had been engaged informally. The marriage would take place in two years. Madaan said that he found all this very strange, but I knew exactly why Bela was doing it.'

The two of them walk down a narrow flight of stairs. There is a reception ahead, consisting of a white desk. A man with an oblong white tilak smeared on his forehead is sitting behind it, talking on the phone. The book rack beside it displays titles on astrology and numerology. The wall behind the reception is adorned with *yantras* of different Gods and Goddesses. A passage to the left leads into an office where the staff is working on their computer terminals and inspecting the reams of horoscopes spooling out of the printers. On the wall above there are calendars and framed pictures of the astrologers of Future Zone being felicitated by famous actors and politicians. There are small rooms behind the reception, separated from the office by a partition. These appear to be the private cubicles of the astrologers.

Sonny interrupts the man at the reception. 'I am looking for consultation.'

The man covers the receiver with one hand and asks politely, 'Who would you like to see?'

'The most accurate astrologer here.'

'Ma'am, all our astrologers are very accurate. If that wasn't the case, we wouldn't be working out of such an expensive office.'

'But who's the most accurate?'

'I am not in a position to say that. But I can tell you that Acharya Krishan is the senior-most.'

'Then I would like to see him.'

'Alright, Ma'am. Please pay us the fee and we'll give you a receipt that you can carry to Acharya's private consultation room.'

'Alright.'

While waiting for the man to prepare a receipt, Sonny whispers in the man's ear, 'Can you tell me about some of Acharya Krishan's predictions?'

The man is taken by surprise and looks blankly at the computer screen for a while before saying, 'Indira Gandhi's assassination. Rajiv Gandhi's assassination. Tendulkar's rise. BJP's rise in politics and many other major predictions.'

Sonny and Ash exchange glances and nod gravely.

'What else?'

The man is about to speak when a slightly effeminate voice interrupts him.

'This year is going to be the wettest in decades.'

The three of them turn around to look at a man dressed in a crisp white kurta and pyjama. He has a round face, with a forehead that juts out. He is short and his big paunch looks more prominent because of the tight-fitting pyjamas. He is chewing on a betel leaf and puckers his lips whenever he sucks in the juice.

'I am Acharya Krishan. I'll be waiting for you in there,' he says, pointing at the first private cubicle behind the reception.

The two of them are standing outside Acharya Krishan's cubicle. Sonny is holding the receipt in her right hand and feeling her pouch with her left. Ash is wondering whether he should knock on the door or simply open it and step in. While he is debating this, Sonny pushes open the door.

The astrologer is sitting on his chair before a nearly empty desk. He has taken off his slippers, which are lying beside him. He has folded his hands, closed his eyes and is reciting a prayer. Sonny and Ash slip inside the room without disturbing the man and quietly take a seat next to him. There is an old, used blackboard attached to the wall, on which two horoscopes are drawn in blue chalk. In the small space below the horoscopes, there is a list of the names of the planets in Hindi and the degree at which they occupy the respective houses of the horoscope. There is a small steel almirah at the back with two brown leather briefcases on top. The table on which Sonny and Ash rest their hands and fidget in nervous anticipation, is bare except for a small brass key, a notepad and a pen.

Acharya Krishan finishes his prayer and clears his throat. He looks at Sonny and Ash intently before he speaks.

'If you are here for the first time, please take a page from this notepad and write down the details of the horoscope you want me to study. If you have already consulted me before, then take this key, open the almirah, take out the topmost briefcase and find your horoscope in one of the red diaries arranged in order of the dates you came to me.'

'I am here for the first time,' Sonny says with a forced smile that hides her growing impatience.

'And who is this? Your son?'

'No. He is my best friend,' she says, rubbing Ash's back as he shifts in his chair uncomfortably.

'Alright, then. Please fill in your birth details in the pages and give me a few minutes to cast the horoscope.'

'Okay.'

Fifteen minutes later, Acharya Krishan has already drawn up her main charts and is taking notes with a pen. Finally, he puts the pen down, picks up the piece of paper and looks at Sonny.

'Ask your question please.'

'Really? Is my chart ready?'

'Yes.'

'Okay. But I hope you don't reveal your clients' details to other astrologers or outsiders.'

'Never, ma'am. We'd be out of business otherwise. Now ask your question, please.'

'I have three questions. One – when is my mother-in-law going to die? Two – when will I find the missing pearl from my necklace? Three – when will a car, a Chevrolet Optra with the number plate DL4C 2010, get stolen or be destroyed in an accident? That's it.'

Acharya Krishan gives Sonny a surprised look and, when she doesn't say anything, turns his gaze on Ash. When Ash gives him a blank, brutal look, he looks down at the chart and starts doodling on it.

After a while, he looks up and asks Sonny, 'Are these the only answers you want? I mean, are these the most important things in your life? Don't you want to know anything about your finances, your relationship with your husband and children, your social standing, your spiritual growth?'

Sonny and Ash look at one another and start laughing. Acharya Krishan feels awkward.

'No,' Sonny says calmly. 'I just want the answers to these three questions.'

'Okay. The chart doesn't show the death of a dear one for another five years.'

'But my mother-in-law is not a dear one. I hardly know her.'

'Ma'am, she's your mother-in-law and, for all practical purposes, a close relation even if you don't feel so. I don't see her death.'

'But she is in a critical condition,' Sonny argues.

'Then she'll stay in the same condition for five more years before passing away peacefully in her sleep.'

'That's not possible.'

'I don't see her death. As for your other two queries, the chart doesn't show any answers for them.''

'What do you mean? I can always ask the jeweller the day and time the pearl necklace was strung. That information can be treated as the date and time of its birth. The place of birth would be the jeweller's shop in Rajouri Garden. I can even get someone to tell me when the Chevrolet Optra was manufactured, though I am not sure if I can ask for its time of birth. The place should be the plant where it was manufactured.'

Acharya Krishan starts laughing and says, 'Your chart shows insanity and a lot of jealousy. It also shows a peculiar mind, a failed married life, failure with your children, and a miserable, disease-stricken old age.'

Acharya Krishan is about to continue when, all of a sudden, Sonny grabs him and gags him with a towel. Ash immediately takes out a bottle of chloroform from his bag and pours a large amount of it on the towel. Acharya Krishan slumps down on the table. Ash checks his heartbeat and breathing to make sure he is alive, then returns the towel and chloroform to his bag. Sonny picks up a duster and a chalk from the blackboard, and carefully studies Acharya Krishan's writing before wiping it clean. She writes something on the blackboard.

When she is finished, she starts shouting and gestures at Ash to follow her example.

The receptionist and four staff members rush to the room and find Sonny and Ash trying to get Acharya Krishan to regain consciousness.

'What happened?' one of them asks.

Sonny starts crying and points to the blackboard on which is written: 'I SAW DEVI IN THIS LADY'S HOROSCOPE. SHE IS A GODDESS.'

One of the staff members calls all the astrologers, and soon the small cubicle is filled with people. While the receptionist is sprinkling water on Acharya Krishan, the staff members and the senior astrologers are taking turns seeking Sonny's blessings. She is sitting on a chair, cross-legged, and placing her hands on the heads of everyone who touches her feet, while exchanging sly smiles with Ash.

'Oh, Ash! It was wonderful, being treated like a goddess,' Sonny exclaims as the two of them are being driven back home.

'I know, Sonny.'

'The Acharya was a big fraud. Wettest year of the decade. It's already February, and it hasn't rained even once.'

Suddenly, huge drops of water start pelting the windscreen, making the driver turn on the wipers. He turns around and tells Sonny and Ash to roll up the windows. They let themselves get soaked in the cold February rain, not speaking a word, digging their nails into one another's palms in fear and worry.

Chapter 7

Sonny is leaning against a blue Maruti Zen parked outside Ash's house. She is dressed in a starched, white salwaar kameez and plain, white sports shoes. She is reading from a newspaper spread out on the hood of the car. After spending a few seconds on the front page, she restlessly starts flipping through the pages before stopping at the obituaries. She stares at the pictures of the newly dead on the page, then takes out a small plastic packet from her pocket. She spills out three passport-sized photos from it onto a corner of the newspaper. Picking up the first photo, she places it over one of the pictures in the obituary column, and steps back to take another look from a distance. She grimaces and tries the second photo. This time, she pulls an even more dreadful face and is about to move on to the last photo, when Ash pats her on her back.

Ash is also dressed in white – white kurta and pyjama, white slippers. He notices the photos of a woman scattered next to the open newspaper.

'Oh, Ash! I'm trying to see which of the three photos of my mother-in-law would look most suitable for her obituary,' Sonny sighs.

'Is she dead, Sonny?' he asks, surprised.

'Not yet, Ash.'

'Then why are you worried about her obituary?'

Sonny walks closer to Ash and wipes a speck of dust from his chin. He turns away in embarrassment. She rolls up the newspaper and hands it over to him. She picks up the small photos from the car and slips them into the small packet, which she returns to her pocket. They start walking. Today, the two of them are not taking their usual route.

During their walk, Sonny tells Ash how her sister-in-law Bela woke up Madaan at four in the morning requesting him to drive down to her place because she had something very important to tell him.

'I pretended to be asleep so that I didn't have to be directly involved in my husband's family politics. He returned in two hours with the same plastic packet in which I had put the three passport-sized photos of my mother-in-law, and woke me up. He looked a little angry and, when I asked him what the matter was, he told me that Bela had another dream last night in which she could clearly see her mother being cremated.

She was sure that her mother had very little time and so she had decided to start making preparations for her funeral. Bela had even called up her elder brother Pramod in London and had got his approval to call up relatives and friends and tell them not to leave town for the next couple of weeks, to start preparing for the prayer meeting and to give Madaan some cash with which he could book an obituary column in a major daily newspaper.

I couldn't control my excitement and asked Madaan if this new dream invalidated her old dream and meant that my mother-in-law wasn't required to visit her elder son in London to attain salvation.

Madaan said it did. I jumped on the bed and quickly opened the packet to see two passport-sized photos of my mother-in-law. She looked ravishing and happy in her early thirties. I lost my temper and told Madaan that I wouldn't let these pictures be used for my mother-in-law's obituary because people would mistake her for a young, healthy woman who still had many years left in her and not realise she was an old invalid who could only find peace in death. Madaan told me that he didn't want the same problems with his mother's obituary as we had with his father's and that, even if some people felt that she still had many years left in her after seeing her picture, they were sure to change their minds when they saw her body. I argued that such people weren't really close family and would never turn up for the cremation. They'd never realise how badly she had needed to die. He told me not to forget that this was just a dream and that Bela had been on anti-depressants ever since she realised that her son would stay away from her.'

'But why does Bela decide which picture to choose for the obituary?' Ash asks.

Sonny starts weeping and tells Ash the real reason for the bitter partition in the family at the time of her father-in-law's death – his obituary which they had published in a leading newspaper.

'Although I still feel guilty for doing what I did, I had no other option. Madaan Chemists was doing very badly at that time and needed some publicity. So when my father-in-law died of a cardiac arrest, I had a brilliant idea. The design and content for the obituary page had come from Pramod. However, he told Madaan to write a suitable RSVP, since he couldn't give his London address. That is when I told Madaan to promote Madaan Chemists by mentioning its address and the tag line, 'The Chemists of

Choice', on the page. Madaan loved my idea but said that we'd be in trouble if Pramod came to know about it. I assured him that his older brother was too busy making money to look for his father's obituary in an Indian newspaper.

So, finally, we went ahead with my idea. Everything seemed to be fine. Even Bela didn't seem to notice the RSVP. Then, on the day of the prayer meeting, Bela took a call from a person who lived in West Delhi, who told her that he had read about Madaan Chemists on the obituary page published the day before and wanted to speak to the owner. He said that he was old and suffering from TB, and hoped that Madaan understood his problems and would be willing to deliver medicines at his doorstep for free. Bela was livid and, although she had handed the phone to Madaan, she went and read the obituary page again.

The next day, after the official mourning was over, Bela faxed the obituary to Pramod who couldn't be there for his father's funeral because his wife was undergoing a gall bladder surgery. That very night, Pramod arrived at our door holding the faxed obituary in one hand and a small suitcase in the other. Madaan tried hard to pacify him but he wouldn't listen. I wondered how Pramod had found the time to fly down to fight when he couldn't make it for his father's funeral. Bela inadvertently let out that his wife was not having surgery. He had been busy attending to a client.

In one week, the shop that Madaan had rented out, and that his brother and sister had tacitly agreed to stay out of because of his financial hardship, was divided into three parts that no one would rent because they were too small.'

'I am so sorry, Sonny. But I think your plan was wonderful. Did it work out?' Ash asks.

'Oh yes, Ash. Business doubled after the obituary was published. But we also lost a major source of income.'

'Honestly, Sonny, I think yesterday was good for you. It means that you'll no longer have to worry about sending your mother-in-law to London. You can now live in peace.'

'No, Ash. Something else happened last night, which really scared me.'

'What was that?'

The two of them see cars parked outside House Number 2. People dressed in white or plain, sombre colours are flocking inside the main gate.

Sonny holds Ash's hand and walks him to shade of a banyan tree. They lean against the trunk as Sonny starts her confession.

'Raghav came and visited his grandmother alone. He told Madaan and me that he was shocked to see her in this condition and had immediately looked up the internet to find out if there was any cure for her condition. He had tracked down two speciality hospitals in New York where this condition could be cured effectively. While Madaan and I looked at each other in horror, he started crying, saying that he wanted to see his grandmother back in good health – this is the same bastard of a grandchild who refused to return from a holiday in Kathmandu when his grandmother had a stroke. He asked Madaan to send him duplicates of her test reports, saying he'd take them with him to New York to check up with the hospitals.

Madaan humoured him at the time, but after Raghav left, he was a mess. After all, we couldn't tell Raghav that we hadn't taken his grandmother to a doctor for the last three years! Madaan knew how mercenary hospitals were nowadays, and if they saw his mother in this state they'd not let her out of the ICU till her last breath. We have already mortgaged our house for Vinod's education. We can't afford to treat a woman who is going to die in a couple of years anyway. What should we do Ash? Should we get the woman treated and stop living our own lives?'

'No. I don't think so.'

'What would you have done?'

Ash stares at the ground and slowly says, 'I don't know, Sonny.'

'It's not good not to know so many things,' Sonny screams and then hugs Ash tight. They stand under the banyan tree, embracing each other, when an old couple interrupts them.

'Excuse me. Are you here for Mr Kumar's funeral?'

Sonny immediately steps away from Ash, wipes her tears and looks at the couple.

'Yes. We are.'

'Was he close to you?'

'Very close. That's why I have been crying.'

'I am really sorry.'

'Me too,' Sonny says, and turns around to look at Ash. As soon as the couple leave, Sonny and Ash start laughing.

'Who is Mr Kumar?' he asks her.

'Must be the man living in House Number 2.'

'You mean you asked me to wear white to attend a stranger's funeral?'

'Yes, Ash. Funerals are educational. They show us many things about a family that we would not find out otherwise.'

Ash laughs. Sonny takes out a bottle of eye drops and a case of shoe shine from her pocket. She tells Ash to put two drops in each eye and then keep them tightly shut for a minute. She also opens the case of shoe shine and rubs some of it under his eyes. Then, the two of them start walking briskly towards House Number 2. Ash wants to know if it is safe to be seen together by people of the colony. Sonny calms him down by saying that it is less a colony and more a collection of houses separated from one another by boundary walls.

They walk inside the Kumars' main gate. Sonny stops briefly to check the name plate. All she sees is the surname and the house number. She has already started disliking the Kumars for not having a more elaborate name plate. She turns around to convey her anger to Ash but he has already gone inside.

The driveway is covered with carpets with white sheets sloppily laid over them. They are marked with dirt and footprints of all shapes and sizes. A few steps on the left lead to a small garden which has a tiny bed of flowers and a wooden swing on which two women are sitting dazed, probably after a long session of crying. The garden looks onto the dining room where, at the centre, an old man's body is lying on two slabs of ice. A male servant is hovering next to the body to mop up the water from the melting ice. The dining area and a cabinet are strangely covered with white sheets. Mattresses are laid on three sides of the body, two against a wall, with some mourners sitting cross-legged and others leaning against cushions.

Sonny takes off her slippers and slowly walks inside. She grabs Ash's hand and the two of them run towards the body, bend down before the uncovered face and start weeping. They look up, see the startled and worried looks on the faces of people and start screaming. Finally, a woman politely lifts Sonny and asks Ash to sit down on the mattress. Ash quietly stands up, looks around and finds a spot next to a lanky boy with dimpled cheeks. Sonny follows him, thanks the woman for supporting her in this dark time and sits down next to Ash.

'Mallika is so considerate, isn't she?' a woman whispers to her.

'Who is Mallika?'

'Mr Kumar's daughter-in-law. Don't you know her?'

'I can't see properly because of my tears!' Sonny blows her nose into a piece of tissue.

'I understand. Are you one of Kumar's relatives? I haven't seen you before.'

'I was very close to him. Please don't ask any more questions. Let me grieve in peace.'

A maid enters the dining room and passes tea around in small Styrofoam cups. When he bends down before Ash, he absently takes a cup and spills tea on his pyjamas and yelps in pain.

'What happened?' Sonny asks.

'He just dropped some tea on himself. It'll be fine. I'll take care of him,' says the boy and takes Ash by the hand. The two of them walk out of the room.

Sonny collects her wits and looks at Mallika sitting right across her, resting her head on an old man's shoulder. She remembers her own father-in-law's funeral – how she was made to run around the house serving old, dying relatives tea and water. She is jealous of Mallika. She sees the brown buttons on her white salwaar kameez and recalls how Bela had made her replace the red buttons from her mourning dress with white buttons at night. She is irritated because Mallika doesn't have to do the work of a daughter-in-law, especially on an occasion like this. Mallika's eyes are not puffed up and don't have dark circles under them. Does this mean that she slept peacefully through the night while her father-in-law's body was lying outside? Sonny feels that's very unjust because, after her own father-in-law's death, the entire family, including her two young sons, was made to sit next to the body and take turns lighting incense sticks.

'Bitch,' Sonny mutters under her breath, looking around for Ash.

He returns holding the young boy's hand, a smile lighting up his face. He can't stop thinking about the way the boy – probably a decade younger than him – asked him to take off his pyjamas and gently wiped the tea stains on his thighs with a wet towel. He even moved his fingers across his thigh to see if there was any rash or swelling. The whole time, Ash felt as if someone was giving him an electric shock. The boy had requested Ash to kiss him. But Ash decided not to oblige so that the boy could feel as deprived and tortured as him.

He sits back next to Sonny, who immediately asks, 'Are you fine, Ash?'

'Yes. Just a mild burning sensation but I can live with it.'

'Are you sure? We can always go to some other cremation. There is no dearth of deaths in this world.'

Ash smiles and looks at the boy who is now sitting across from him with a spiteful look on his face.

'Yes, Sonny. I am fine. Let us take this to its logical conclusion.'

'And what would that be?'

'Nuisance,' Ash exclaims, smiling.

Sonny is about to respond when the woman sitting behind her, probably under the impression that Sonny was close to the elder Kumar, starts whispering in her ear. 'Do you know why the dining table and the cabinets are covered?'

Sonny moves back till she is right next to the woman. 'Now I feel lighter. Crying so much has made me feel better. What were you saying about the dining table and the cabinets?'

The woman shifts closer to Sonny and goes on. 'The senior Mr Kumar, as you know, was a hale and hearty person who detested going for medical check-ups or having medicines. He was perfectly fit. He was also a shrewd businessman and doing well in the construction business. However, both his sons were the complete opposite. The elder son, although married, with a healthy six-year-old daughter, suffered from chronic epilepsy and was, at the moment, drugged and put to sleep so that his condition didn't worsen from seeing his father's dead body and cremation. The younger son had idolised his father and wanted to have a construction business as successful as his father's. With the help of his father's money, contacts and goodwill, he had built a small construction empire of his own, but that crumbled after two years and he had to declare his company bankrupt. Till his last days, the senior Mr Kumar was running the household all by himself.

A few months ago, the younger son fell in love with a girl from a very rich family. Her parents even came and met the Kumars. When they asked to meet the boy's siblings, Mr Kumar told them that he just had one brother who had died during child birth and now only a mad cousin from his maternal side lived with them, since no one was willing to take care of him. When they asked the boy what he did for a living, he told them that he was managing his father's business and was solely responsible for bringing it to such great heights.

The senior Mr Kumar knew very well that he couldn't get a girl from a richer family, and the political connections of the girl's father would help him get construction permits and contracts from the government. After days of silence, the girl's father called up Mr Kumar and told him that he was ready to marry his daughter into his house – but only because of him and his status as a businessman.

The marriage is scheduled for next week. The boy lost his mother years ago and had, just hours before the senior Mr Kumar's cardiac arrest, taken a heavy dowry from the girl's family during a *shagun* ceremony. Now, the boy has decided not to inform his prospective in-laws of his father's death. He will tell them that his father has been hospitalised. He has also decided to get married to the girl secretly for fear of being exposed as a failed businessman and losing the entire dowry. The girl has fallen for him and is ready to build a life with a struggling man, but she is also aware that the wedding will be cancelled if her father comes to know of Mr Kumar's death.'

'So, what's on the dining table and the cabinets?'

The woman hesitates for a while before saying, 'All the dowry!'

'Really?' Sonny asks, feeling a burst of excitement inside her.

'Yes. They didn't have the time to put away the stuff.'

'I'll be back in a minute,' she tells the woman and drags herself close to Ash.

'Ash! Ash! I know what we have to do now.'

'What?'

Sonny points at a little girl dressed in a pink frock, sitting in the garden, playing with a doll.

'Who is she?'

'She is Mr Kumar's granddaughter.'

'How do you know?'

'She had come over to our house with her maid, once, to get medicines for her father.'

'And what are we going to do with her?'

'Just wait and watch, Ash.'

The two of them go to the garden. Sonny looks around and makes sure they are alone, then quietly whispers to the little girl.

'Come here, sweet child. What's your name?'

The girl looks up blankly.

'Come here. I'll tell you something about your grandfather.'

The girl's face immediately lights up. She drops the doll and comes running to Sonny and Ash. Sonny makes her sit down on the stairs, looks at Ash, and then asks, 'What has happened to your grandfather?'

'He is doing his morning *kriya*,' the girl says innocently.

'Who told you?'

'My mother.'

'What will happen after the kriya?'

'She said that grandfather will be going for a long meditation course to the hills and will write me letters.'

'Really?' Sonny laughs.

'Yes.'

'What if I tell you that the man lying down in the dining room is not your grandfather and that your real grandfather is hiding on top of the dining table? What will you do then?'

'I'll remove the sheets, find him and scold him!'

'Then do that.'

'Promise me I'll find him.'

'Promise.'

Sonny and Ash stand on the steps and strain their ears. Suddenly, they hear the girl scream her lungs out saying, 'Where is my grandfather? He is not on the table!'

Soon they hear a loud slap and the girl's loud cries. A woman, probably her mother, tries to calm everybody down by saying that her daughter couldn't sleep the whole night and was getting cranky. The mourners start whispering. One of them stands up and asks, 'What is all this?'

Sonny and Ash quietly sneak out of the house. Standing outside Ash's gate, Sonny wipes off the shoe shine from under his eyes and asks him, 'Had fun today?'

'Lots!' he says.

Chapter 8

Sonny and Ash are seated at the far end of the small eating area in the GR Hospital canteen. There is a wash basin at the right and a counter at the front, with cardboard cut-outs of special treats dangling from the top. It's a self-service place. One of the staff members emerges from behind the counter at regular intervals and clears the tables.

There is an eerie silence, some people are staring blankly at their plates or fiddling with disposable spoons and forks, while others whisper into their cell phones, giving updates to worried relatives or discussing prescriptions and medical reports. Those who are eating don't talk, concentrating on their meal to get momentary respite from the trauma of a loved one's suffering. Most of the food is left half-eaten.

Today there are several patients inside the eating area, (oddly christened Food Court) – an old woman in a wheelchair who is being spoon fed, a teenage boy with a cast on his hand being made to sip mango juice by his mother, a child with gaping holes on his wrists from which a tube is emerging, slowly biting into a black forest pastry.

Sonny is feeling jealous at the way the families are treating their sick relatives. She coughs excessively to see if people notice her, but nobody does, except for Ash. She smiles at him and tells him to continue eating. Sonny thinks that, perhaps, she too should fall sick so that her family and her world would take notice of her and consider her special. She is mentally ticking off some illnesses that could land her a prolonged treatment and turn her into the centre of attention.

She has rejected AIDS because it has no cure. She is not sure whether she should have tuberculosis of the lungs or the spine, so she keeps her options open. She has ticked off first-stage cancer because it can be treated easily. She has rejected brain haemorrhage or a mental illness because she doesn't want to end up like her mother-in-law, unaware of the attention being showered on her. She doesn't want any gynaecological illness because that would embarrass men and she'd lose out on a large number of sympathisers. She doesn't mind having an illness that is hard to pronounce or considered rare as that would make everyone wonder about it and, consequently, about her. She will accept an accident if her car doesn't need too much repair, or if the accident was caused by another driver who'd have to pay her compensation. She has already decided to buy a new car with that money and sell off the old car after getting it repaired.

Ash is fantasising about being bedridden in one of the hospital rooms and being visited by a handsome, male doctor who will check his abdominal injury. During one such examination, while his pants are down and the doctor is looking at the injury, Ash will pee on him. He'd love to see him run out for a wet towel, come back and wipe his abdomen in gentle strokes. Once he has recovered and the doctor has fallen in love with him, he'll visit his house while his wife and children are out. The two will play a game where, every time one of them pees on the other's body, he'll be allowed to take off a piece of clothing from the other's body. After hours of peeing on each other, whoever gets the other one naked first will get to be the master during sex.

'Ash, try the gravy of the *shahi* paneer. It's delicious.'

'I think I'll just have the daal, Sonny.'

Sonny grabs Ash's spoon from his hands, fills it with the steaming gravy and holds it out before his mouth. Ash looks a little embarrassed but Sonny insists, nudging the spoon near his mouth so that the gravy starts dripping. He immediately laps up the gravy, biting down so hard on the spoon that it gets slightly disfigured.

'How was it, Ash?'

'Sour.'

'I like it sour. Do you?'

'Yes. But why are you avoiding the paneer in the gravy, Sonny?'

'It's very bland. They don't cook it, but just put the raw chunks in the gravy once it's done.'

'You sound as if you know what's going on in the kitchen.'

'Oh yes, Ash! How wouldn't I?'

'What do you mean?'

'Well, my mother-in-law was admitted to this hospital when she had her first stroke. It was a very trying time for the family.'

'But what has that got to do with the menu of the hospital canteen?'

Sonny looks around to see if anyone's listening. Then, mixing some of the gravy in the rice, she brings her face close to Ash's and whispers.

'When my mother-in-law had a stroke, I first thought that she was just feigning it so that Madaan and I wouldn't go on a holiday to Mauritius. But once we got her to the hospital, we realised that it was serious. She was kept in the ICU and we shared a cramped room next to hers with Pramod and Bela. Pramod ate the food Bela's driver used to get from her house every day. I had told Madaan that I wouldn't have my meal at the same time as them. Madaan discussed this with Bela and the two came up with a timetable that they drew up on a chart and hung on the wall. We all followed the timetable, with Madaan and me eating dinner slightly early and Bela and Pramod a little late.

A very sad thing happened when my mother-in-law was in the hospital. Nandan, our servant of five years, who became a favourite of my mother-in-law's in a very short time, decided to quit and go back to his family's farm in Himachal. I pleaded with him not to go, but he was adamant. Later, I learnt that he had left because he couldn't stand seeing my mother-in-law die a slow death. I was faced with a dilemma. Madaan had requested me to cook for him and our sons. I was used to being pampered by Nandan and hadn't stepped into the kitchen for a long time. When I refused, Madaan told me that I'd then have to do with the hospital food as the canteen food would turn out to be too expensive. I agreed, relieved that I wouldn't have to cook all day for the family. It was only after eating the insipid hospital food that I realised I had made a big mistake. Moreover, I was jealous of seeing Bela and Pramod eat elaborate feasts. When I complained to Madaan that the food was barely edible, he said that he had no problems with it and that, if I did, I could go home and cook for myself.

One day, while Madaan was busy doing the children's homework after they were back from school, I went to the hospital canteen. Although it was very small and different from the Food Court of today, the *thali* was more or less the same. I couldn't resist tasting the food and found out that it was much better than the hospital food. That is when I befriended a young waiter there, telling him that I was the wife of the Ambassador of Mauritius and that, if he could secretly supply me the canteen food in my room, I would pay him in Mauritian rupees, which was worth ten times the Indian rupee. I also promised to hire him to work in my villa when my husband was discharged from the hospital. The boy was taken in. The same day, he bribed one of the nurses in the hospital kitchen and secretly served me the canteen meals. Ash, I always knew that the unused currency I had saved up would come in handy one day.

On the day my mother-in-law was going to be discharged, I called up the reception and complained about the boy and the nurse, telling the receptionist that they were trying to give normal food to my mother-in-law. When she asked me why they would do that, I said that the boy's father held a grudge against the Madaan family since he had been an employee of my father-in-law's before being thrown out unceremoniously. One week later, when I came to the canteen once again to savour the food, especially the shahi paneer, while my mother-in-law was at home, I couldn't find the boy anywhere.

Oh, Ash! I ate almost a hundred meals for those Mauritian currency notes biting the dust in our safe.'

'Wow, Sonny! How do you get away with all this?'

'Like we have been getting away with our pranks, Ash.'

The two of them stand up and walk towards the counter. A waiter is emptying the steaming daal into a dish from a large, circular, steel container. He keeps the container back on the floor and picks up another one, full of steaming rice. At first he tries to simply let it fall out, but most of the grains stick together in clumps. He then takes a big spoon and quickly scrapes the rice out. Then, he uses the back of the spoon to level the rice. He looks up to see Sonny and Ash standing before him with plates in their hands. He nods indifferently.

'We'd like some more gravy,' Sonny says, smiling.

'Ma'am, this is not a buffet. You'll have to get a slip from the payment counter.'

'Even for a few spoons of gravy?'

'Yes.'

Sonny pinches Ash in the back and he immediately starts coughing. She keeps her plate on the counter and holds Ash, who has started coughing uncontrollably.

'It's okay, Ash,' she says. 'I know you have very little time left. But why would this world care?'

The waiter is looking at Ash with concern and asks, 'Very little time? How? He looks healthy.'

'No. He has terminal leukaemia. After two years in the hospital, the doctor finally gave us permission to take him home and let him die peacefully. I promised him one last, normal meal at the canteen before he goes back home and starts following the prescribed diet.'

'But he doesn't look like he is sick,' the waiter argues.

'That's because the hospital staff took great care of him, giving him his medicines on time.'

When the waiter looks unconvinced she adds, 'Or do you doubt the expertise of your own doctors?'

'No, Ma'am! Not at all.'

'Seems like it. But never mind. We'll get the slip made. Ash will just have to exert himself. How does that matter to you?'

The man looks down in contrition and asks Sonny to hand over the plate. She does so instantly. He fills up the plate with gravy. He then smiles at Ash and asks him to hand him his plate. He fills that up with gravy too. The two of them are about to turn around and go to their seats again when the man tells Ash to wait. He goes inside the kitchen and comes out with a glass of fresh juice.

'Have this. You'll feel better.'

'Thanks,' Ash says between coughs.

The two of them are about to finish their meal when Sonny says, 'Ash, if you want more then you can ask the man. I am sure he'll give you all you want.'

'No, Sonny. I can feel a pain in my chest from all the fake coughing.'

'But, Ash, remember – no pain, no gain.'

'I know, Sonny.'

The two are about to resume their conversation, when a young woman holding a baby in her arms sits down next to them. She buries the baby's head inside her red blouse and starts rocking on the chair. Sonny grimaces while Ash simply looks away from her, waiting for Sonny to say something. The woman looks around from time to time, adjusting the baby's mouth on her nipple.

'Let's go, Ash.'

'Why?'

'I get nausea when I see a woman breastfeeding. It brings back very bad memories of my first delivery.'

'You mean Gaurav?'

'Yes.'

'You never talk to me about him.'

'What's there to say? He is still studying and doesn't bother us for money.'

'Then how is he a loser?'

'Well, because he didn't clear any of his medical entrance exams and we had to pay a hefty sum for his admission. Then we had to bribe the third-rate medical institute to promote him when he flunked his first year exams. It's just that Vinod is a greater burden on us. Also, Gaurav is very quiet and doesn't talk much.'

'Alright.'

'If you're suffering from both cancer and a seasonal cold, you are bound to worry about the cancer more,' Sonny adds.

'I agree, Sonny.'

As they walk out of the Food Court, Sonny recalls the torture she had to endure the first time she breastfed Gaurav.

'He sucked on my nipples so hard that, by the time he was sated, they were swollen and red. I complained to Madaan about him but my in-laws said that I would have to feed the boy for eight months, as advised by the doctors, and then gradually wean him. I controlled my rage, but when I was discharged from the hospital and alone in my room with the infant, I tried to feed him cow's milk. When Gaurav didn't cry after drinking it and went off to sleep, I decided to tell Madaan that I had used a suction pump to empty my breasts and feed Gaurav. Sadly, an hour later he vomited. After cleaning him up, I tried to feed him cow's milk again but he threw up again. I gave in and decided to breastfeed the boy when I got a call from my mother.

My younger sister had got engaged and the ceremony was to take place in two weeks. She told me that the groom's family wanted the engagement to take place two days after both the families had agreed on the match, but she had told them about my delivery and that she would like me to recover fully and be present at the function. Now I had another reason not to breastfeed Gaurav – I didn't want my breasts to sag and look bad at my sister's engagement ceremony. That's when I decided to try Payal's milk on Gaurav. Payal was our two-year-old Alsatian bitch, who had just given birth to five pups.

Milking Payal wasn't difficult. One day, when Madaan and my in-laws had gone out I called Payal to my bedside and tied her up with a rope. Then I put a container under her teats, massaged them and, slowly, started milking her. Once I was through, I tried her milk on Gaurav. Luckily, Gaurav didn't throw up, and so I continued to feed him the bitch's milk for another month. After a month, Gaurav started drinking cow's milk. In the process of milking Payal, though, two of her pups died of malnutrition and Payal turned wild. So I told Madaan to sell the remaining pups and put down Payal because she had become a danger to the children. Madaan packed her off to an animal shelter.'

'So how did the engagement go?' Ash asks.

'Really well Ash. Everyone including my sister's fiancé was ogling at me. I didn't have the heart to tell Anjali that she was going to marry a man who lusted after her elder sister.'

'Where is Anjali now, Sonny?'

'We've lost touch, Ash.'

'And your parents?'

'They died in a car crash near Pragati Maidan. Ironically, they were driving down to the Bhairon Baba Temple to offer liquor to the god so that my younger sister's financial condition could improve.'

'I am so sorry Sonny! I wish you had told me about the tragedy.'

'What tragedy? The tragedy is that they married me off to a loser just because they had great regard for his father. The tragedy is that Bhairon Baba enjoyed the brand so much that Anjali is now rolling in millions.'

'Really?'

'She is a dental surgeon in the US. Her husband was fired from his job and started a web portal from home. He sold it off for millions and now they are living in a posh mansion in California. She tried keeping in touch but her newly acquired wealth gets on my nerves.'

'I can understand, Sonny.'

'Anyway, I am sure it's some adult dating portal. Like I said, the man had lust in his eyes.'

'I agree, Sonny. Also, geniuses are not fired from their jobs.'

'Exactly, Ash!'

The two of them leave the Food Court and settle down on a small ledge right outside Das Pharmacy. They stare at the patients and their relatives swarming inside the small, suffocating pharmacy, stuffed with boxes of medicines.

'Brisk business, Ash,' Sonny says spitefully. 'It pays to have a pharmacy inside a hospital.'

'I can see that, Sonny.'

'And look at Madaan Chemists. It's on a narrow lane, in a residential colony, flanked by houses. We are not strategically located.

I had asked Madaan about selling Madaan Chemists and buying out Bela's and Pramod's shares in his father's shop. He was quite upbeat about the idea and called up Bela, but that bitch said that she'd like to use her portion of the shop to build a memorial for her father. I told Madaan that his father was just a good doctor and not Elvis Presley, but he didn't have the guts to confront Bela.'

'But what would have you done with the whole shop?' Ash asks.

'We would have made it part-clinic and part-chemist's store. We'd have put a local physician on our payroll and asked him to write long prescriptions for patients. Sadar Bazaar has many gullible people since they are not well educated. You can't do the same thing with the shrewd businessmen in Mansarovar Garden.'

'Oh! Sonny. I am so sorry.'

'I know, Ash. However hard I try, I can't come up with a solution to make more money for my husband and our loser sons, so that I can enjoy life.'

They spend the next half hour or so eavesdropping on worried relatives and patients making frantic calls to doctors. Whenever Sonny catches a glimpse of a long prescription or overhears a relative or patient divulge bad news, she finds some comfort and advises Ash to do the same.

'That's how cruel the world is,' Sonny says philosophically.

'True, Sonny,' Ash replies.

'So, Sonny. Does Madaan ever ask about us?'

'No, Ash. He is much too stressed out about our loser sons. He knows only about our walks, not the trips. Whenever I call the cab and the two of us leave, it's after I've had a long fight with Madaan over his mother, our sons or his brother and sister. I tell him that I need a break.'

The two have decided to go on a tour of the emergency ward, when an ambulance with a blaring siren halts near them. The driver immediately steps out and rushes to the back. He opens the door, revealing a badly bruised, bleeding leg falling over the edge of a stretcher. A woman with a cut on her lip and over her right eyebrow gets out and starts looking around, waving frantically. Sonny and Ash get a sudden adrenalin rush and run towards the ambulance door. They see a boy with a battered face and bruised body wincing on the stretcher and screaming loudly as the driver, the woman and the hospital staff take the stretcher out. They rush indoors. Sonny and Ash run along with them.

Sonny is looking at the boy's face. He is screaming and contorting his face in pain. Sonny is worried that the boy may be suffering more than her and Ash. But she assures herself that his pain is mostly physical and that their pain is mental. Physical pain is easily treatable while the latter is not. So, even though on the face of it, everyone would say that the boy is suffering more than them, it is Sonny with a failed marriage, failed children and a failed social life, and Ash with his mental illness and pent up rage who are suffering infinitely more. Ash is looking at the area around the boy's crotch, covered with a blood-soaked sheet.

People in the corridors look at the stretcher with horror and make way for it. They enter the ward which is filled with patients and relatives. One of the staff members leaves the stretcher and starts running ahead, pointing towards the emergency room.

The two of them have been sitting next to the woman in the waiting room for the last fifteen minutes. She hasn't spoken a word to them and has been weeping quietly. Finally, Sonny breaks the silence.

'What happened to him?'

'Suicide attempt,' she says, the words barely audible.

'And how did you get hurt?'

'He almost fell on me while jumping from the third story of his apartment. His hand hit my face. I don't even know who he is except that he lives all alone in the apartment and is not from Delhi.'

'I see.'

Sonny gets her a cup of coffee from the vending machine. She takes a few sips and then leaves the cup under her seat. One of the staff members comes out of the room and tells the woman that the boy is asking for his father.

'Please, will you come along with me? I feel very awkward going in by myself,' the woman tells Sonny.

'Yes,' Sonny and Ash chorus.

'Thank you so much. I don't know why I had to be involved in this. I probably should have eaten my breakfast at home. That way I would have saved myself from being a part of this horrible spectacle.'

Sonny puts an arm around her and the three of them follow the staff member inside the ward.

An antiseptic smell hits them as they enter the emergency ward. The corners are lined with makeshift beds surrounded by doctors and nurses checking their patients' vital signs, adjusting drips, or simply pulling up blankets that have fallen down to their knee or ankles. As they make their way down the aisle, Sonny hears the relative of a patient complaining to one of the doctors that he had been promised bed space for his son, who had been hospitalised three days earlier.

The boy is lying on the bed directly facing the entrance. A nurse is monitoring his vital signs, while a young attendant is trying to adjust a bandage across his forehead. The moment he sees them he squints and asks, 'Who are you?'

'I am Sonny. This is the woman who brought you to the hospital. And this is my friend Ash.'

'Okay. Please can you come a little closer?'

The woman is about to walk ahead when Sonny stops her, squeezes her hand and gets closer to the boy along with Ash. The two of them pull up two plastic chairs and sit down.

'Tell me. What happened?'

'I defaulted on two monthly installments. The loan recovery agents finally came home and confiscated my house and car. Now I am left with nothing and I have two aged parents to fend for.'

'Where do you work?'

'For a software company.'

'What is your designation?'

'Senior accountant.'

Sonny looks around to see if the woman is within hearing distance and says, 'What is the best bank to go to for an EMI policy?'

'Sorry?'

The boy raises himself slightly on the pillow but falls back again. 'Why are you asking me now?' he says, grimacing in pain.

'Because I want a car. And I'd like to get it on installments. Since I don't want to end up like you, I'd like to know which bank sent the recovery agents.'

'STI,' the boy says.

'You mean the other banks don't have recovery agents?'

'All of them do. But this bank hires goons to recover its money. The other recovery agents are civil people.'

'Oh! Okay.'

'I'm sure you were saved to give me this piece of information,' Sonny smiles.

'What do you mean?'

'Forget it. Tell me – any other precautions that I should take before getting a loan?'

'I am sorry, but I am feeling miserable right now,' the boy says.

Sonny comes closer to him and whispers, 'I am miserable too, being driven around in an outdated car, so please tell me – any other precautions?'

While Sonny is talking to him, Ash slips his hand under the sheet and starts massaging the boy's feet. All he can feel is bandages, fresh bruises, goo and tangled hair. His hand gets bloody. He wipes the blood on the bed sheet and stares at the boy again.

'Tell me!' Sonny says angrily.

The boy gives Sonny a shocked look and then asks for the nurse. Sonny immediately stands up and Ash follows her.

The woman stops them on their way to the entrance and asks, 'What did he tell you? What were you telling him?'

'Oh, nothing. Just that trying to kill oneself is against the Almighty's wishes. Isn't it, Ash?'

Ash nods.

'Oh! You two are wonderful, really! All this help for a stranger.'

'Thank you so much. Now we need to go. We're late for our doctor's appointment.'

'Which doctor and which room? Maybe I can join you afterwards.'

'I am sorry. Not today. Ash is unwell and we might need to get some tests done.'

'Alright. Thanks again.'

On their way to the door, Sonny says angrily, 'Today's mission was a failure, Ash. We couldn't do anything.'

'That's probably because a lot has already been done to these poor people.'

'Yes. That could be true. Anyway, I really enjoyed my meal at the canteen.'

'Me too, Sonny.'

Chapter 9

'The girl will look good in this. What do you think, Ash?' Sonny holds up a pink dress.

'Isn't it too big for a seven-year-old?'

'I can't make her wear a tight-fitting dress. Her wounds have swollen and they will stand out.'

'Then take it, Sonny.'

'Give me two of these in the same colour,' she tells the seller.

'Would you like anything else?' he asks, as he tosses the two crumpled dresses at a young assistant and asks him to pack them.

'Do you have belts?' Sonny asks.

'For men, women, or unisex?'

'An all-purpose belt.'

'Sorry Ma'am. We only have belts for women.'

'Can I see them?'

'Sure.'

The man ducks under the wooden table at his small, open-air shop, and takes out a few sleek belts.

'Oh, forget it!' Sonny shouts, making a face at him.

'Why, Ma'am?'

'They're too light and won't serve my purpose.'

'At least try them on, Ma'am.'

'What makes you think I'll buy a belt for myself from this cheap shop?' Sonny asks, enraged.

'I don't know Ma'am. You just bought two dresses...'

'They were for my maid.'

'Okay. We don't keep track of whom our customers are making their purchases for,' the man smiles.

'Are you joking?'

'Forget it, Sonny. Just take the dresses,' Ash says, holding her hand.

'Alright, Ash. But it's only because of you that I'm not doing anything.'

Sonny grabs her package and the two of them walk away.

Today, they are at the P. Bazaar Shopping Complex, in front of an endless row of open-air stalls at the entrance of the parking lot, where new and used clothes are being sold.

There is a prepaid auto stand at the front with a queue of auto rickshaws, some empty, others with drivers napping inside. The pavement is crowded with ice cream carts improvised to sell mineral water, soft drinks and eatables. Hawkers are obsequiously following the crowd, mostly families on vacation and youngsters, and trying to sell their wares ranging from fake Ray-Ban sunglasses and fake sports bags, to electric hairbrushes and statues of the laughing Buddha. A tourist couple laden with shopping bags is standing before the florist's, right next to the security check post, getting their picture clicked by a professional photographer.

The hawker selling hairbrushes stops in front of Sonny and Ash. He switches the hairbrush on, and starts running it through his hair.

'Very good for calming your nerves,' he says.

At first, Sonny looks disinterested, but a glance at Ash changes her mind.

'How much?' she asks.

'Two hundred only!'

'One hundred and fifty,' she replies.

'One hundred and ninety,' he says.

'One hundred and sixty,' she says, prompting Ash to start walking so that the man is forced to follow them.

'One hundred and eight five.'

'One hundred and sixty five,' Sonny laughs.

'One hundred and eighty, final!' the man says, controlling his anger.

'One hundred and seventy. Final,' Sonny says.

'Alright.'

Sonny is nervous and nudges Ash so he starts walking faster. The man speeds up his pace and continues to follow them. The moment the two reach the security check, Sonny points the man out to a female security guard behind the metal detector. She gives the man a cold stare and he immediately turns back, shaking his head.

They are standing outside York, the only eatery in the basement. The front counter displays cold and stale chow mein, burgers, bread rolls, patties and rice and manchurian.

Sonny is sipping almond milk, Ash is drinking cold coffee with ice cream. The two are quietly enjoying the argument between a middle-aged woman and the man at the counter. The middle-aged woman had asked for just cold coffee but the man had added a scoop of vanilla ice cream to it. When the man told her that she'd have to pay thirty rupees extra for it, she became livid. She said she had just asked for cold coffee. The man pointed at a small sticker on the refrigerator full of cold coffee, almond and strawberry milk saying: 'Cold coffee will only be served with ice cream.' 'This is cheating,' the woman says and wants her money back. The man tells her that she should have read the sticker. Sonny hopes that the woman is fighting over the ice cream not because she has to pay extra but because she has a bad throat. Ash is happy that he likes cold coffee with ice cream. Finally, the woman pays the man for the ice cream, but then makes a great show of throwing it in the dustbin and leaves.

'Madaan should do the same,' Sonny says.

'What?'

'Make it compulsory for customers to buy one medicine with another.'

'And how would that work, Sonny?'

'Medicines that kill the side-effects of stronger medicines?'

'But that's illegal.'

'Who's saying that he needs to paste a sticker? He can always convey the condition to the customer.'

'Hmm.'

Sonny smiles at Ash.

'Why the two new dresses for the maid, Sonny?' Ash asks. 'I thought you hated her and that's why you beat her up so mercilessly.'

Sonny swallows some almond milk, lowers the bottle and says, 'It's because of my mother-in-law, Ash. An old friend of Madaan's is coming to visit us today.'

'What? But you told me that you had stopped inviting friends over, so that they couldn't find out about your financial condition.'

'I had to make an exception in this case, Ash.'

'Why?'

'Two days ago, Madaan returned from the store earlier than usual. I was sleeping soundly in my room, tired from the bath I had given my mother-in-law that morning. Just then, Madaan's cell phone started ringing. I remembered Madaan telling me about a man who was willing to rent our ground floor for three years. Fearing it might be him, and that I'd annoy him by not taking the call, I answered.

To my utter dismay, it was Lalit, an old school friend of Madaan's who wasn't well off. We exchanged pleasantries and I told him that he could try calling Madaan at dinner time. He asked me about my mother-in-law. The moment I told him that she was in very bad shape and could die any day, he burst into tears.

Lalit told me that his mother, who was widowed at a very young age, was suffering from cancer of the spine. It had been four years now, and the cancer had spread all over her body. She wasn't even able to eat and had started looking like a skeleton. Still, he had decided to use his savings and get her admitted to a hospital in Delhi so that the doctors could try to reduce her pain. I tried to empathise with him, but then he said the unthinkable – that he had not seen anyone who was suffering so much and needed to be taken away by God.

I immediately started shouting at him, telling him never to make such assumptions. At least, not when my own mother-in-law was alive. I told him how my mother-in-law was the sickest person in the entire world and needed to be taken away by God more than anybody else. Lalit said that he was in touch with Madaan, and he had never mentioned that she was so sick. I wanted to scream at Madaan! I told Lalit that no son would be willing to say that his mother could find peace only in death, but that I was honest. Lalit continued to protest, saying that it was difficult to imagine anyone sicker than his mother. After all, what could be worse than terminal cancer and a body weight of thirty kilos? I became nervous – my mother-in-law was fifteen kilos heavier. Finally, since we were not able to reach an agreement, I told Lalit to come over and see my mother-in-law. I also told him to get some new pictures of his mother so that I could see if she was really suffering as much as he claimed. At first he was taken aback by my request, but then he agreed.'

'I hope I did the right thing, Ash?'

'Absolutely, Sonny. Let Lalit see for himself.'

'He's in for a rude shock,' Sonny starts laughing, leaving her bottle of almond milk on top of a crate stacked against a wall.

Ash also finishes his drink and the two of them start walking past the shops. They stand outside an electronics shop, staring at a video game in which an oriental man is remorselessly punching a hairy beast. With every punch, the beast spits out some blood. The caption 'Press Start' is blinking on the screen and, in the background, there seems to be a dungeon. Two controllers are lying idle on a table in front of the screen. At first, Ash is hesitant, but a polite nod from the man inside encourages him to go up to the console. Sonny follows him, happy that he is taking some initiative. Ash is looking closely at the screen, as he chooses two players for a fight. Ash is Sonya and the computer is Liu – the same oriental man who had first attracted Ash's attention.

The fight has started and Liu is steadily kicking and punching Sonya. She is consistently spitting blood, staggering, falling and then getting back on her feet. Ash is not doing anything except moving Sonya forward, towards Liu, and waiting for him to come close to her. Every time he does so, Sonya gets beaten up. Finally, Sonya loses the battle and Liu somersaults in triumph.

'Why didn't you put up a fight, Ash?' Sonny asks, disconcerted. 'Let me take Liu. Then we'll fight.'

'Okay.'

Both Sonny and Ash are struggling with the controls, although Ash is more comfortable. All he's doing is making Sonya rub her body against Liu's or bend before his tight crotch. Sonny can't understand what he's trying to do. Sonny makes Liu punch Sonya and shouts at Ash to fight back, but he only brings Sonya closer to Liu and simply has her stand next to Liu, or rub against his body. Finally, frustrated, Sonny leaves the remote and tells Ash to stop playing. Ash turns back from the console, nods to the salesman outside and follows Sonny to the spiral staircase.

They are standing at a counter in one of the movie stores on the first floor. A young man is taking out piles of DVDs, while Sonny and Ash look at him expectantly. Finally, a young boy walks in carrying DVDs from a door on the side, hidden behind a poster. Both of them can see different naked body parts on it – pink, purple, cream, brown and black. The man coughs to get their attention. He takes the pile from the boy's hands and dumps it on the counter. He holds up each DVD, showing Sonny and Ash the covers.

Sonny looks away and blindly grabs the pile. She asks Ash to pick up any two DVDs.

The man interrupts, 'But their quality differs, Ma'am. At least see what you are going to buy.'

'It's not for me!' Sonny shouts.

'Then let sir here see them,' he says, pointing at Ash.

'It's not for him either.'

'Okay. None of my business.'

Ash takes out two DVDs and hands them over to the man. He takes the cover off them and slips them into plastic cases. He then puts them inside a black polythene bag and hands them over.

'How much?' Sonny asks.

'Two hundred.'

Sonny gives him the money and they are about to leave when Sonny looks at the man who showed her the DVDs and says, 'You think I am foolish enough to believe that those were real breasts?'

'What?'

'The ones on the cover.'

'Yes, they are,' the man says, embarrassed.

'All that this world wants to do is to try and prove that I am not woman enough!'

'Ma'am?'

'Never mind,' she says and hands over the polythene bag to Ash.

As they walk down the stairs, Ash asks Sonny, 'Who are these movies for?'

'Bahadur.'

'You mean the colony's night-guard?'

'Yes, Ash. The same Bahadur.'

'Are you having an affair with him?' Ash asks, moving back a little.

'Oh no, Ash! You should know me enough by now not to ask such a foolish question.'

'Then what are the movies for?'

'Bahadur recently got married, back in his village in Nepal. Now he is back with his wife and staying in rented quarters at an army officer's house. I was surprised when he confessed to me that he didn't know how to have sex. He knows about my family problems and we both confide in each other. Actually, I grew fond of him ever since he helped me a great deal in trying to trace Jerry. A few days ago, Bahadur asked me if there were any movies that could teach him how to have sex. That very night, I looked everywhere in my sons' old room and finally found a scratched porn DVD with the visiting card of this shop in P. Bazaar. That is one of the reasons we are here today.'

'But why would you want to indulge a night watchman, Sonny?'

'Last week, there was a robbery in House Number 13. One TV and 20,000 in cash was stolen. Bahadur was not on duty that night. He told me that burglars from the nearby slums were using the sewer to reach the houses and that they had their eye on this colony as many businessmen live here. That is when I made a deal with Bahadur. I told him to guard only my house at night and let the burglars steal everything from the other houses. In return, I'd get him movies to educate him about having sex with his wife. He said that he might lose his job because of that, but I told him that there was nothing more shameful for a young man than not knowing how to have sex with his new bride. He agreed, although he did warn me that he'd occasionally guard the other houses too. I told him he could guard them, but not prevent them from being robbed. He agreed.'

'Great, Sonny!'

'Oh, Ash!' Sonny suddenly starts trembling.

'What happened, Sonny?'

'I forgot to tell him to guard your house!' She starts crying hysterically.

'That's okay, Sonny. We have our personal guard.'

'Then it's fine,' she says, relieved, and embraces Ash.

They start walking towards the exit when a young man with belts dangling from his hands stands right in front of them.

'Pure leather at a very cheap price, Ma'am. Please have a look.'

Sonny looks at Ash and the two of them reach a silent agreement.

'Actually, we are getting late. Could you please accompany us to the underground parking lot with the belts? We'll try them there,' Sonny says.

The boy seems a little baffled. Sonny takes out some Mauritian rupees from her purse and starts counting the money.

'Shopping is so much fun in India, Ash, isn't it? Especially when the Indian rupee is so cheap compared to ours,' she says.

'I know, Sonny.'

'By the way, how much have we spent on our shopping trip this time?'

'I think, three lakh rupees...'

'Only three lakhs? Sonny exclaims, looking at the boy, who smiles meekly.

'Yes. Last time it was five lakhs, Sonny.'

'You mean we have two more lakhs?' she asks, going closer to the boy and looking past him at his small, corner shop.

'Yes.'

'Just give me five minutes. I'll get all my stock and get someone to watch over my shop,' the boy says eagerly.

Soon, he follows them as they walk briskly through the dark, poorly ventilated parking lot. His entire stock of belts is hanging from his shoulders. Sonny is looking at the scooters and the motorcycles parked to her left behind the pillars. The pillars are marked with letters and numbers painted in red. Some of them have exit signs on them, with arrows pointing to the right. Others have instructions like 'no spitting inside the parking lot', and 'two wheeler drivers are responsible for their helmets' written on a board. Ash is looking at a grill fencing in front, which seems to be the only source of light in the dingy basement, apart from the flickering tube lights in the engineers' offices on the far right. He can see two electronics shops behind the offices. In the corner is a malfunctioning elevator, doors open, littered with rubble and refuse.

Suddenly, a motorcycle whizzes past them, barely missing Sonny. She almost falls back, but Ash manages to hold her. They see two youngsters wearing Manchester United T-shirts stopping the bike and looking back at them. The driver is smirking, while the one sitting behind shows them the middle finger. Sonny is about to run after them when Ash grabs her hand. The two look at each other, turn back to look at the boy with the belts who hasn't noticed the insult, and look back at each other in disgust.

They reach a narrow lane crammed with cars, far away from the engineers' offices and the payment booth. Sonny stops at a Toyota Corolla, turns around to look at the boy. She asks Ash to keep an eye out for anyone, and gestures to the boy to stop.

'Is that your car?' he asks politely, taking off the belts from his shoulders and keeping them on the ground.

'Yes. It is.'

'It looks very expensive.'

'You mind your own business and show me the belts.'

The boy bends down to pick up a few belts from the ground. Just as he is about to stand up, he is surprised to find Ash hovering over him.

'So, you'll try first?' he asks.

Ash doesn't say a word and waits for Sonny to speak.

'Actually, we want to use the belts for beating people.'

'What?' the boy asks, shocked.

'Yes. In our country, we use belts to beats thieves, liars and petty criminals. Crime rates have increased and I would like to gift my husband, a police officer, these imported belts.'

'Oh! So you want a hard belt?'

'Yes,' Sonny says.

'Then you should go for this suede belt with metal loops. It will hurt a lot.'

'Actually, we'll need to see that for ourselves. I don't want my husband not to like the gift. You know how finicky police officers are. Are you willing to take a few lashes?'

The boy looks around, and then at Sonny and at Ash. Both of them are smiling. He is about to pick up all the belts and turn back, when Sonny deliberately drops a wad of one rupee Mauritian notes on the ground.

The boy stares at it and looks embarrassed before saying, 'Okay. But I'll take a hundred rupees extra.'

'That's no issue,' Sonny says.

He hands over the suede belt to Sonny and stands before her. He closes his eyes and says, 'You can try it on me.'

'Thank you.'

'But are you sure you'll buy my belts?'

'Of course.'

Sonny unleashes the belt and cracks it in the air a few times. She then looks at the young boy and hits him on his arm. He trembles and screws up his face. Sonny starts reminding herself of all her family and financial problems and hits the boy again, this time with greater force. He turns his face away in pain but stays rooted to the ground. He asks Sonny to continue. Sonny is in tears when she remembers how her mother-in-law is still alive, how her sister-in-law is richer than her, how Madaan doesn't even touch her, and how her two sons can't find employment. She hits the boy again. However, it is the recent insult by the two young boys that adds fuel to the fire of her hatred, and she strikes the boy once again, the buckle landing on his right cheek and leaving a red scar at once. He clenches his fists and begs Sonny to go easy. She starts breathing heavily, tired from the physical exertion, and hands over the belt to Ash. Ash whispers something into her ear before getting into position.

Sonny moves away and tells the boy, 'Please scream the moment the belt lands on you.'

'Like this?' the boy asks, letting out a low squeal.

'A manly scream.'

'But I am just a boy.'

'It should be like a grunt.'

'Can you give me an example?'

Ash immediately grunts like a man enjoying an orgasm.

'Okay,' the boy says.

Ash moves his hands back and lashes the belt at the boy, hitting his chin. The boy grunts. Ash adjusts his penis and slaps his thighs together to hide his erection. He hits the boy again and the boy grunts again, feebly this time and not to Ash's liking. Ash doubles up the belt, walks closer to the boy and hits him on his back.

Just when Ash starts feeling a strong sensation gripping him down under, the boy says, 'Go slow sir. I am not a criminal although I can say this is quite a punishment.'

Not happy that the boy's words have disturbed his rhythm, Ash moves back and, after a nod from Sonny, strikes the boy with all his might. The belt lands on the bridge of his nose. He covers his face with his hands, falls down and starts screaming. Sonny and Ash drop the belt, leave a few Mauritian rupees next to the boy and start running away. The boy looks up at them from between his fingers and starts shouting.

'You bastards! Where are you running? Give me my money!'

Sonny and Ash are sitting inside a Maruti Alto in 'Underground Level 3' of the parking lot. The boy was found by two police officers and the three of them are on the lookout for Sonny and Ash.

They couldn't find any open cars to hide in at the first two levels. On the third level, they found a Maruti Alto with its doors unlocked. They jumped in, locked the car from inside and knelt down at the back.

'Fun, wasn't it, Ash?'

'I know. But what if we get caught?'

'Don't worry. The parking lot is too big.'

Just then, they hear the boy's shrill voice. Sonny takes a peek and sees the boy walking past, followed by two policemen.

'Bend down, Ash,' she whispers frantically.

It's been an hour since they heard the boy's voice. The two of them have fallen asleep, Sonny's head nestled between Ash's sweaty, wiry arms. Suddenly, Ash feels something wet and sticky. He looks down to see that Sonny has gently folded up his T-shirt and is sucking on his stomach. He jerks back on the seat, pushing away Sonny's head from his body.

'Sorry, Ash,' she says.

Ash doesn't say anything and takes out a piece of tissue from the dashboard. He starts wiping Sonny's spit off his T-shirt and skin.

'Ash. Do you love me?' she asks, facing him.

He is quiet.

'Tell me, Ash.'

He looks at her blankly, then looks down again. He scrunches the tissue up and drops it under the seat.

Sonny touches Ash's cheek and is about to kiss him when he grabs hold of her shoulders so hard that she screams. He asks her not to move while he takes out the two pink dresses from the shopping bag. He puts one over Sonny's head, violently, and makes a tight knot of the two sleeves. He asks her whether she can breathe. She says she can but only through her mouth. 'That's enough,' he says.

She starts begging Ash to tell her what he's up to, but he tells her to stay quiet. He then taps her heavy breasts. They jiggle like two big lumps of jelly. He takes out the second dress and ties it around her chest, trying to flatten her breasts as much as he can.

He turns her towards him and sees a faceless creature with a slight bulge on its chest. He is happy that they don't look like breasts any more. He then takes out some tissue papers from the dashboard and rolls them up. He unties Sonny's pyjamas and stuffs the tissue inside her panties.

Sonny is groping in the darkness, trying to see through the dress. Finally, accepting that she has no choice but to play along with Ash's fantasy, she says, 'So Ash. What firm were you working for?'

'It was a men's lifestyle magazine.'

'In print?'

'No. Online.'

'And why did you leave it?'

'Because my boss saw me writing something unacceptable in one of the dumb cheat sheets we were preparing for our idiot readers.'

'What do you mean?'

'We were writing about how men could save themselves from possessive girlfriends.'

'What did you write?'

'I wrote, 'Kill that stinking bitch' in red letters.'

'And they fired you for that?'

'Yes, Sonny. I couldn't lie to them and say I'd written it in jest,' he says, stroking the rolled up tissue papers that have gone soft with sweat.

'Ash, what do you do the entire day?'

'I spend time with you, Sonny. Otherwise I just sleep or play with my dogs. My father doesn't allow me to go out at night or step outside the city – not even to a relative's place. So the time I spend with you is all the time I have outside.'

'What does your father do?'

'He's a small-time businessman.'

'And your mother?'

'A bored housewife.'

'Brother?'

'Regular guy. Likes partying, fucking and watching movies. It's a very regular family.'

Sonny wants to ask him why he attempted suicide but cannot muster the courage. 'What are your dogs named, Ash?' she asks instead.

'Buzo and Bingo.'

'I'm sure Jerry would have loved Buzo and Bingo,' Sonny says.

'I'm sure too, Sonny.'

'So what should we do now?' Sonny says, after Ash has taken the dress off her head, and untied her chest. When he moves his hand inside her panties, she says, 'Let it stay there Ash. I'll keep it safe, away from this cruel world.'

'Let's leave,' Ash says.

The two of them get out of the car, but not before Sonny steals a car freshener and a fountain pen from the glove compartment. They shut the door and look at each other with a great sense of relief. As Sonny passes by the Maruti Alto, she drags the tip of the fountain pen hard against its body, leaving a long silver scratch in her wake.

Chapter 10

Sonny and Ash are sitting on a soft, downy sofa in the lobby of Hotel Le M. Guests, mostly European and Japanese tourists, are flitting around followed by the desperate, ingratiating hotel staff: the men dressed in white shirts, black trousers and coats and shiny black shoes, their hands folded conspicuously against their stomachs; the women in saris whispering to one another. The two of them are looking at the long panel of rectangular mirrors on top which clearly reflect the beauty treatment shop, the business centre and a silver stand with square holders containing lighted candles. They are sitting right in front of the conference area, consisting of a table surrounded by swivel chairs, each with a glass, a sealed bottle of mineral water, a notepad and a sharpened pencil lying on it. At the centre of the table, there are two crystal bowls – one with cookies and the other with boiled sweets wrapped in plastic.

'Oh, Ash! I'm glad that India has started showing signs of a recession,' Sonny says.

'Why?'

'Sales at Madaan Chemists have doubled. My husband is selling ten times the anti-depressants, sleeping pills and condoms he used to sell a month ago.'

'Condoms?' Ash asks, looking a bit surprised.

'Don't worry, Ash. Nobody is having sex. Some men just have to display their manliness by standing at a medicine counter and asking for condoms. But I don't know why their sales have grown tenfold.'

'Maybe they want to show the world that they can get an erection even when work is stressful and money is tight?' Ash suggests.

'Yes, Ash. That could be it. In fact, I am sure that *is* the reason.'

'You must be happy, Sonny. Finally your husband is making money.'

Sonny shakes her head in disgust before saying, 'No, Ash. He still has doubts over selling sleeping pills without a prescription. We have a customer, a woman, who buys five strips of a very expensive sleeping pill every two weeks. One day, Madaan came home worried that she was very depressed and might try taking an overdose. I gave him a scolding for worrying about a stranger's depression, reminding him of my post-natal depression after Vinod's birth and how he had never done anything more than getting a strip of anti-depressants from his shop every week. He said that it was not her depression that was worrying him as much as the possibility of her dying after the overdose and the police investigating him. I calmed him down by saying that nothing could stop the woman from dying if she wanted to end her life. I also reminded him how Bela's best friend's daughter, an aspiring model, died when broken glass from a window overlooking the poolside of a hotel fell on her, splitting her head in two. When Madaan didn't understand the connection, I told him that if she was meant to die from sleeping pills purchased from Madaan

Chemists, nothing could be done about it. What do you think, Ash? Did I do the right thing?'

'Absolutely, Sonny. Anyway, these sleeping pills hardly kill you. At most, the woman will need a lavage and a few weeks of bed rest.'

'Exactly, Ash. I am really sickened by Madaan's lack of business acumen. Had I been in his place, I would have started cultivating the woman, referred her to a psychiatrist I know, and taken a cut on every session she had with him. But my idiotic husband gets wrapped up in such small things. It's strange, really.'

'I know, Sonny,' Ash commiserates with her.

Suddenly the two of them hear a commotion at the entrance. Two women employees are standing right next to it with steel thalis in their hand. The manager is standing before the door, holding two marigold garlands. The moment a middle-aged, well-groomed couple steps inside, the man greets them heartily and garlands them. The two foreigners look visibly embarrassed but bow gently in gratitude and fold their hands. One of the staff members puts a *tika* on their foreheads, while the other starts sprinkling rose petals on them.

Sonny looks at Ash, disgusted, and says, 'They are not welcoming a couple but foreign currency. Isn't that pathetic, Ash? Our own people are starving to death, or having to sit in the reception area like the two of us, and these bastards are busy sucking up to strangers from a faraway land.'

'I know. It's really sad, Sonny.'

The couple walks towards the reception with almost half the hotel staff following close behind. The woman says something to the man and he simply nods, motioning her to the empty sofa next to Sonny and Ash. She kisses him on his lips, leaves the luggage and heads towards the two of them.

Sonny looks at Ash and shouts, 'Hurry Ash. Hide your right hand inside your shirt.'

'Why?'

'Just hide it!'

Ash hides his right hand inside the sleeve of his shirt, his elbow straining against the cloth.

'Is that okay, Sonny?'

'Absolutely, Ash. Just stay like this for a while longer.'

The woman sits next to the two of them, and starts reading a travel guide on India. She is about to turn the page when Sonny clears her throat and says, 'Looks beautiful, but it isn't.'

'Pardon me?' the woman says in heavily accented English.

'This country you are visiting Madam. It looks beautiful in books, but it isn't.'

The woman shuts the book and sets it down on the table. She shifts in her seat anxiously before looking at Sonny, narrowing her eyes and asking, 'What do you mean?'

Sonny takes out a plastic packet from her handbag and hands it over to the woman. When the woman hesitates, Sonny grabs her hand and presses the packet hard against her palm.

'What is this?'

'See for yourself, Madam.'

She slowly opens the packet and takes out some folded newspaper cuttings. She keeps the packet down and slowly starts unfolding the old, creased scraps. She opens the first and looks shocked. It reads: 'Terror Ravages Delhi Again. Thirty Dead.'

She opens the second.

'Posh South Delhi Market Struck By Terror. Forty Die.'

The third.

'Delhi: The New Terror Hub. Five Terrorists Killed In An Overnight Encounter With The Police.'

The woman meticulously folds the newspaper cuttings, puts them back in the packet and takes a deep breath. She looks at Sonny.

'I know about these terror strikes. But our trip organiser told us that after the last attack in Delhi, security has been stepped up and tourists have nothing to worry about.'

'They always say that,' Sonny laughs.

'What do you mean?'

'They don't care about your safety, Madam. All they care about is your money.'

'I am afraid he is a very considerate man. Anyway, how it is your business to warn tourists coming to India, and that too at a hotel lobby?'

Sonny looks down and starts sobbing. The woman looks at her with genuine concern, wanting to console her but not knowing how. Finally, she takes out a tissue from her purse and hands it to Sonny who takes it without even looking up and blows her nose. Ash is trying hard to control his laughter, pressing his right hand hard against his stomach to make sure that it doesn't move.

'I am really sorry, but would you mind telling me what's on your mind?'

Sonny looks at Ash and asks him to shift so that the woman can see him.

'Who is he?'

'He is my son.'

'Okay. And?'

'He lost his right arm in a terror strike last year.'

'Oh, Christ! That's awful. I am very sorry.'

'But that's not the end of it, Madam. I lost one of my sons in a terror strike six months ago.'

'Oh dear. You make this country sound like a war zone.'

'It *is* a war zone, Madam. We are surrounded by countries run by terrorists. How long can we remain free of their influence?'

'You mean Pakistan?'

'Yes. And all the other countries bordering India.'

'I don't know. Our trip organiser was saying just the opposite.'

'All of them are part of a nexus. And that includes the Ministry.'

'You mean the Indian Government?'

'Yes, Madam.'

'And may I ask you how you know all this?'

'I worked for an NGO, Madam, and these were our findings.'

'Oh, Christ!' the woman says, clutching her chest and taking deep, measured breaths.

'Do you think it'll be safe for us to stay in this hotel for one night and then fly out to London tomorrow?'

'No, Madam.'

'Why?'

'Because Le M is on the hit list of all terrorist organisations operating in South East Asia.'

'But why?'

'Because this hotel has a restaurant which our prime minister visits every two weeks to have his favourite meal. The terrorists want to blow him up, along with the building.'

'Oh no!' the woman says, pressing her hands against her temples.

Soon, she regains her composure and takes the garland off her neck and throws it on the floor. She ferrets through her purse and takes out a compact. She snaps it open and looks into the mirror. She starts wiping off the *tika* from her forehead, muttering abuses under her breath and blaming a man named Tom, probably her husband, for not reading up about India's situation and, especially, about the hotel being on the terrorists' hit list.

'Taj Mahal! All that he ever wants is to see that damned tomb, not thinking that we could lose our lives doing it!' she tells Sonny.

'That's not his fault, Madam. Is it, my son?'

'No,' Ash says.

The woman takes a visiting card from her purse and says, 'This is my business card. I am a senior recruiter at a major UK firm. If you need any help please feel free to call me. I am Ellen. You?'

'Sonny,' she says excitedly, looking at the card. 'You probably don't know Vinod Madaan, do you?'

'Who is he?'

'He is the brightest MBA student in India.'

'Is he related to you?'

'Yes, he is my youngest son.'

'I see. He must be from one of the IIMs, or the International Business School in Hyderabad?'

'Oh, Ellen! I feel so bad for you. You have no idea about India.'

'What do you mean?'

'The best MBA school is in Mumbai, where Vinod is currently pursuing his MBA.'

'We've recruited from one college in Mumbai, but that is certainly not the best,' Ellen argues.

'This college is on the outskirts of Mumbai and has the best faculty, curriculum and the greatest success stories.'

'What's it called?'

'You wouldn't have heard of it – but it is certainly better than the colleges you mentioned.'

'The lists and all the news stories can't be false, can they?'

'They might not be. But the media have been asked not to praise this college because the owner's younger son is a journalist who published an exposé on the ruling party.'

'Oh, this is too hard for me to follow!'

The woman picks up her purse, bids Sonny goodbye and starts walking towards her husband who is holding out a credit card before one of the staff members.

'Ash, hurry! Let's hide inside the bathrooms till the couple leaves.'

'Should I put my hand back where it belongs?' Ash sniggers.

'Not till you are in the bathroom.'

Sonny and Ash are sitting on a different sofa. Ash has uncovered his arm. The two are looking at the reception where the manager and the hotel staff have gathered to discuss something in muted tones. They look disconcerted. The manager breaks away from the group and walks towards the entrance. He instructs a sweeper to mop the floor littered with rose petals and vermilion powder. He tightens his tie, shakes his head and walks back to the reception where an argument has broken out between two staff members. Sonny looks around to see Ellen and her husband, but can't find them. Ash is rubbing his right arm which feels slightly stiff. The two of them keep watching the entrance in case they see Ellen and her husband again.

After half-an-hour or so, Sonny finally breaks the silence by saying, 'I think our trick worked, Ash.'

'I think so too.'

Sonny's cell phone starts ringing, playing the tune from the latest Shahrukh Khan movie. Sonny stares blankly at the screen and holds the cell phone out as if she wants people around her to hear the tune. When she sees nobody is interested, she disconnects the call and looks at Ash.

'Who was it Sonny?' Ash asks.

'Oh! It was Madaan.'

'Then why didn't you take his call?'

'Because he didn't want to speak to me.'

'Then why was he calling?'

Sonny moves closer to Ash and says, 'We have a silent agreement that whenever one of us leaves the house, the other person will call at least once. Usually, the person who is outdoors sends an SMS saying that this is the best time to call and impress the people in whose company we are at that point. We have saved the latest songs as our ringtones. Madaan and I think that if people hear our ringtones, they'll feel that we keep ourselves up to date.'

Ash covers his mouth with his hand and starts laughing.

'What to do, Ash? We can't dress according to the latest fashion trends or drive around in fancy cars, so we have to do what we can to stay fashionable.'

'I understand,' Ash says.

The phone rings again, but this time Sonny disconnects as soon as she sees the name of the caller on the screen.

'Who was it Sonny?'

'That loser, Vinod.'

'What does he want?'

'Money. What else Ash? I've already laid out the conditions for him if he wants us to fund his stay in Mumbai.'

'What are they?' Ash asks.

'Vinod had called earlier today. The bastard didn't even have the courtesy to greet me and asked straight away why the demand draft hadn't reached him. I was enraged. I told him that now that he was doing his internship and was being paid a small stipend, he could pay his rent and the maid's wages on his own. Vinod was shocked and told me that, because of the meltdown, he wasn't being paid any stipend and the firm he worked for had only agreed to pay for his travel and food. I told him that it was not my fault that he hadn't got admission to a better college and, consequently, an internship with a firm that paid him a proper stipend.

But I finally agreed to tell Madaan to send the demand draft on two conditions. One – Vinod would sign a legal document stating that he had no claim on our house. Two – he'll get married within two years to a rich woman so that I can use the dowry money to buy two brand new cars and get the house renovated. Vinod started crying, asking me what I was planning on doing with the house if I didn't leave it to him or Gaurav? I said I'd give it on rent and shift to a smaller house in a posh colony. Vinod agreed to my first condition but said that Madaan might not want him to sign any document. I said I'd convince him. Vinod told me that he was already going out with a very sweet, homely girl from a middle-class family, and that he loved her very much. I told him that he'd have to break up with her immediately and start looking for a girl from a rich family. I wouldn't mind if she was not good-looking, not well-educated, had health problems, or was handicapped even. All I wanted was my return for taking care of him for twenty four years. Vinod agreed and told me to ask Madaan to send the demand draft. Maybe he was calling to discuss the conditions again...'

'Did I do the right thing, Ash?'

'Of course, Sonny. You can't look after Vinod for the rest of your life, can you?'

'Exactly, Ash.'

'Ashwin!'

Sonny and Ash look up to see a handsome young man dressed in a polo T-shirt and track pants, holding a black, Nike equipment bag. Before the two of them can react, the man drops his bag on the floor and hugs Ash tight. Ash tries to escape from the embrace by jabbing his chin on the man's shoulders.

'Ouch! Ashwin, that hurts.'

'He's Ash. Not Ashwin. You are mistaken,' Sonny says vehemently.

'Ash is his nickname. Ashwin is his real name.'

'Is that true Ash?' Sonny turns around to look at Ash, unable to hide her shock.

'Yes, Sonny. But very few people know that.'

'You could have told me, Ash.'

'It's not important what my parents named me, Sonny. How can these things affect our relationship?'

'Relationship!' The young man exclaims picking up his bag. 'Ashwin. Are you in a relationship with her?'

'We're very close friends, Akki.'

'Akki is short for Akshit,' the man tells Sonny. 'Anyway, Ash. What are the two of you doing here?'

'Oh! We're waiting for a friend to join us for lunch at the coffee shop.'

'That friend is standing right in front of you! Ashwin's oldest, dearest friend from school.'

Ash looks around uncomfortably before saying, 'Yes, Akshit.'

'So, what are we waiting for? Let's go.'

'Sure, Akshit.'

The three of them sit at a table right at the entrance of the coffee shop. Akshit is hungrily eating his fish and chips and sipping his cold coffee, while Sonny and Ash are taking small bites from their salad and exchanging nervous glances.

Akshit points a fork with a chunk of fried fish at Ash and says, 'What've you been up to, dude?'

'I am writing a book.'

'What book?'

'About a troubled boy.'

'I hope it's not your autobiography.'

'Ash is not troubled at all! He is one of the happiest people I know,' Sonny interrupts.

Akshit takes a bite of the fish and starts laughing, 'Who are you trying to fool, Ma'am? I was there at the hospital when he was being treated for a massive overdose.'

'Oh! That was just a mistake. Wasn't it, Ash?' Sonny feigns a smile and starts rubbing Ash's back. He doesn't say anything and stares blankly at the salad on his plate.

'Of course not. Ash fell into depression after the eighth grade. Strange, since that was the year when all of us discovered porn and masturbation. I always wanted to know why he had grown so quiet but he never said a word.'

'What else?' Sonny says as Ash slaps her on her thigh.

'He attempted suicide on the day I was going to propose to a girl. I am still going out with her. It's been nine years now, and we plan to marry next year. That day, I had called Ash up in the morning, asking him to come to Ego at Friends Colony. All our common friends told me that my efforts would go in vain, but I still called up for old times sake.'

'What old times?'

'We've known each other since nursery school. We have very fond memories of school, our adventures on school trips. And our secrets.'

'Okay,' Sonny says.

'Anyway, Ash, have you found a girl for yourself?'

Ash continues to stare at his plate.

'Dude! Get a girlfriend and all your depression and suicidal thoughts will vanish. After your suicide attempt, I had also begun to wonder about the whole point of existence. I even thought you may have done the right thing. If my long-time girlfriend was not by my side, maybe I would have done the same thing as you.'

Ash doesn't say a word.

'I am serious. You're so good-looking. You just have to make the right moves.'

'Yes. Ash is gorgeous!' Sonny exclaims.

'Sonny. Why don't you tell Ash to get a girl?'

Sonny gives Akshit a hard stare so he immediately turns his gaze to Ash.

'Listen Ash. I know many girls who'd be willing to satisfy your deepest, darkest desires. What is your favourite girlfriend fantasy?'

Ash picks up the fork and stabs it into the salad. Sonny is looking anxious.

'Don't tell me that you don't have a girlfriend fantasy, Ash. All guys do!'

Ash pushes his chair back and is about to stand up when Sonny shoves him back and pulls the chair forward.

'Have you still not felt up a woman's boobs, Ash?' Akshit laughs.

Ash freezes.

'Ash! Do you even know what a vagina looks like?'

Suddenly Ash looks up, clenches his fist and punches himself hard on his face. The whole table shakes and a glass of water crashes. Water slowly seeps all over the table cloth and starts dripping on to the floor. Akshit and Sonny stand up and walk towards Ash who is holding his mouth with both hands, blood trickling through the gaps between his fingers.

'Ash! What have you done?' Akshit screams.

The whole room is staring at them. Two waiters rush to help Akshit hold Ash up. A woman employee comes running to their side, asking if she should call for a doctor.

'No. It'll be alright,' Sonny tells her.

Akshit carries Ash in his arms, his white polo shirt soaked in fresh, red blood. He turns around and tells Sonny, 'I'm taking him to the bathroom. He has lost two teeth and that's why he is bleeding.'

Sonny starts crying, drops into her seat and requests the waiter to clear the table.

Half an hour later, when Akshit and Ash still haven't returned, Sonny decides to go to the bathroom. She hesitates outside the gents' bathroom for a while, then slowly opens the door and walks in. She sees the bathroom attendant mopping up blood stains from the floor. On her right, two towels soaked in blood are lying next to a case of Le M shoe shine and tubes of moisturisers. On the wall above, a flat screen TV is playing Tom and Jerry cartoons.

Sonny walks up to the wash basin, opens the tap and starts washing her face. She is about to pull a towel off the rack and wipe her face when she see one of Ash's teeth lying next to the wash basin. She looks around to find the other tooth, but can't. She goes back to the table angled under the television set and rummages under the towels and tubes. Finally, she looks at the attendant and asks, 'Where are the two boys?'

He points towards a large door with a wheelchair sign on it.

Sonny walks towards it and opens it slightly.

She covers her face with her hand and retches, seeing a swollen-faced Ash hung on the handles meant for handicapped users and Akshit with his pants down, penetrating him from behind. Ash is swaying his head in pain and ecstasy, while Akshit grunts with every thrust. Sonny rushes back to the wash basin, but not before she hears Ash squeal out her name.

She cleans herself up, hurriedly, and runs out.

Part III
Sonny

Chapter 1

Sonny was very reluctant to be a part of the organisation. She knew very little about such people and refused to consider herself one of them. All this time, she had been living a life of denial. Suddenly, she had no option but to confront this bunch of strangers who had nothing in common with her except a quirk.

Before calling up the man who had accosted them at the park, she had gone to Ash's house one last time in the hope of catching a glimpse of him. She stood on the pavement, staring up at the balcony, hoping that the door would open and he would step outside. She considered the possibility of walking past the main gate, going inside, and asking his parents how he was doing. After all, she hadn't slept a second since the night Bahadur, her loyal guard, had come rushing to the door informing her that he had seen an ambulance leave House Number 8. Had Ash done it again? she wondered.

For days she tried to go for walks by herself, but felt empty and scattered without him. As days turned into weeks, the realisation dawned on her that Ash had not only been a perpetrator of their acts, but also the inspiration behind them. His presence, she felt, had rationalised all that she had been doing.

She hadn't heard from him since that day.

It took her a long time to get over his physical loss. Mentally, she knew she could never be rid of him.

One day, she accidentally came across the organisation's card while cleaning her purse and decided to give the man a call. He gave her directions to their headquarters and a suitable time to meet him and the other members. She felt as if the man was smirking while talking to her. Before hanging up, she wanted to tell the man about Ash and that, in a way, she was being forced to come to the organisation. But she also felt that this was her only chance to regain a part of her life without which she had started feeling so lost.

The HQ is a house on the main road, in a posh South Delhi colony. It is flanked by two embassies done up beautifully, with tall, imposing gates, a security picket outside and the country's flag fluttering gently in the breeze. As she reaches the gate, a man hops off a parked motorcycle on which he had been perched, chatting with a few other locals. He asks her where she wants to go.

She does what she was told to do. 'The Watcher's Club,' she says.

He nods quietly, opens the gate and tells her to go to the basement. As she walks past the driveway, she sees a young foreigner. She is sucking on a lollipop, staring down at Sonny from the first-floor balcony. Further up, are two more floors, both probably occupied by foreigners.

As soon as she takes the marble stairs to the basement, the light starts fading. She grips the wooden railing hard, her eyes closed, her palms sweaty. She tries to imagine Ash standing right next to her to boost her confidence.

Soon, she is at the door. The knob is shaped like a brass angel. She is about to knock when she hears the sound of thunderous applause from inside. She fears an onslaught of strangers trying to make her feel uncomfortable with their questions. She is already forming a mental image of a group of fashionable young couples staring at her, when the door opens and the man extends his hand out to her.

As she enters, she sees a young girl squatting and staring at a huge mirror held up before her by two young men. To the left, there is a wooden sliding door leading to a huge room. On the right, she sees people sitting on wrought iron chairs, light sofas, bean bags. An old man on a wheelchair is there too, his visibly abashed wife or partner standing right behind him. There is a glass table next to the seated people. It is covered with cameras, photo albums and stacks of CDs. Even before Sonny can manage to make eye contact with everyone, the girl squeals and starts urinating. The puddle of urine between her feet slowly starts spreading sideways. The girl looks at the mirror, everyone looks at her. Having finished what seems to be her solo act, the girl pulls her panties and short skirt back on and walks proudly towards the gathering. The man looks at her approvingly.

'Who's next?' he asks.

Sonny takes a seat next to the man on the wheelchair and his wife. A young man gets up from his seat, holding a clump of blonde hair in his right hand. He stands before the puddle of urine and starts speaking.

'Blonde hair turns me on more than blonde women do. I love watching blonde hair. For the last two years, I have been going to upscale movie theatres which screen English films. I make sure the theatre is relatively empty. Once the movie has started, I shuffle between the seats till I reach a seat right behind a blonde woman. Then I slowly lift her hair and snip it. In two years, after collecting more than twenty samples of blonde hair, I think I should be made a member of Watchers.' He smiles, craving the crowd's approval, but he only gets a grave look from the audience.

The young man comes back from his position near the puddle and stands before the gathering.

'Is he a Watcher? Yes or no?'

'Yes!' the gathering shouts in unison.

The man looks at the thrilled boy and says, 'Congratulations Anil! You are now formally a member of Watchers. Please furnish all your details to us during our next session.' The boy jumps up and down in delight, waving at the gathering.

'Who's next?' the man asks, dampening the young boy's jubilation.

The woman standing next to the man on the wheelchair raises her hand. Everyone looks at her. At that moment, they also glance at Sonny, who shifts in her chair uncomfortably.

The woman stands near the pool of urine along with her wheelchair-bound husband. She looks at the man for her cue to begin. He nods.

'Rajan and I haven't had sex in twenty years. Yes, twenty years! I don't blame him entirely. After our daughter's messy divorce, I lost all interest in sex. Even though now she is happily married again and has two healthy sons, I just couldn't recover from the shock. Maybe it was because of my first son-in-law, whom I had taken a great liking to. Rajan never complained about my lack of sexual appetite. In fact, he had asked for my permission to have sex with other women. For the sake of keeping our marriage together, I let him. It didn't make much of a difference to me. Then, Rajan met with an accident that paralysed him. He was bedridden for three months after which we placed him on a wheelchair. The moment my daughter brought him out of the room on a wheelchair, I couldn't take my eyes off Rajan. I started watching him while he watched TV, while he ate, or chatted with his old friends. Then, one night, I told Rajan that I was aroused, seeing him on the wheelchair. He was taken aback, but told me that we could have sex. I said I just liked watching him. That's it.'

The woman ends her speech and wheels the man back to the empty spot next to Sonny, who looks at her without any surprise. This is nothing compared to what we have done, she thinks.

The man stands back, facing the gathering.

'Is she a Watcher?'

'Yeeeeeees!' everyone screams in unison.

'There you have it, Anjali ji.'

'Thank you so much,' she says to the man. Her husband wipes a tear from his eye.

After two prospective members are refused entry to the club and everyone has taken a break for refreshments, Sonny and the man are the only two people left in the room.

'You must watch the movie we've made,' he says.

'Where?'

He points to the wooden sliding door. 'There's a small home theatre behind it, with seating arrangements for up to thirty.'

'Okay.'

'When do you plan to become a member?'

'Will I have to do what all these people did?'

'Yes. That's the rule.'

'Then, the answer's no. I just want to know if you can find me a young boy who'd be willing to go out for walks and occasional trips to different parts of Delhi with me.'

'Doing what?'

'Just being with me. Like an assistant.'

The man tells her to wait and disappears into the room past the sliding door. He returns with a pile of files.

'You can go through these and find a suitable candidate. They're all very intelligent, highly educated young boys and girls, desperately looking to earn some money.'

'Where do you get these from?'

'We were looking for volunteers – web designers, content writers, film editors – for the movie we've made.'

'And how do you plan to screen your movie?' Sonny asks, curious.

'Oh! Didn't I tell you about watchers.com?'

'What's that?'

'Our internet community. It's members-only, of course – you have to pay a substantial amount. At first glance, it looks like an innocent site for bird watchers, full of exquisite shots of exotic birds. But once you enter the site as a member, you can find out everything about us.'

'I see. But why would you want to help me? I'm not even pretty,' Sonny asks him, feeling her rough cheeks and looking down at her bulging waist.

'Because I understand your need.'

'How?'

'We are not born like this. We are just not in control of our lives. These activities – they make us feel otherwise. They return to us a measure of control. They are our solace.'

'Whatever,' Sonny says and grabs the files from his hand.

She pores over the résumés for about an hour, before finally selecting Akhil. She notes down his contact details on a piece of paper, thanks the man and leaves, hoping that Akhil will turn out to be as good as Ash. Or even better.

Chapter 2

Sonny meets Akhil around noon.

She is late by one hour. He is standing outside Ash's house, his hands nervously slipping in and out of his trouser pockets. She walks up to him and smiles. He tries to look her in the eye but gets intimidated after a few seconds. She takes a neatly folded piece of paper from her pyjama pockets and hands it to him. He gives her a puzzled look but, when she stares at him coldly, he puts the paper in his pocket without saying a word.

The two of them start their walk, Sonny staying behind Akhil to see if he is capable of taking initiative. While crossing Ash's house, she stops briefly to look up at the balcony, but doesn't see anything except for pigeons pecking madly at their reflections on the glass panes and shitting on the walls. She is about to stop and find solace in the birds' distress when Akhil speaks.

'Yay, Sonny! The Chevrolet finally got bashed up.'

For the first time since losing Ash to Akki, Sonny sees a ray of hope.

She walks up to Akhil who is standing next to a tree and looking at the bashed bumper of the Chevrolet outside House Number 10. She shrieks in delight and wonders if her two second-hand cars look better compared to the damaged Chevrolet. They do. And that makes Sonny feel very relieved. She pats Akhil on the back for his discovery.

The two are about to resume their walk when Sonny sees a Delhi number plate dangling from the back of the damaged Chevrolet. Which means that this is not their friend's Chevrolet, but theirs. And if they have the money to buy a brand new Chevrolet, they might even have the money to repair it. Sonny is heartbroken and thinks that Akhil should have checked the number plate before declaring victory. After all, she had taken one whole hour to brief him about the walk and what he was expected to do.

They pass House Number 10. Sonny hopes that the owners are compelled to drive the damaged car to a party or a place where she and Madaan, too, are present with one of their second-hand cars. That way, people would forgive her for not buying a new car and focus their attention on the Chevrolet.

They see a tent being pitched outside House Number 12. People are rushing in and out of it, carrying chairs, tables, lights, garlands, containers, cutlery and coiled electricity wires. Sonny immediately looks across the road to see two men fixing a green generator to provide backup for the celebration at night. She nudges Akhil. He looks at her questioningly. She loses her temper and nudges him again.

'What, Sonny?' he asks.

'Don't you see the tent and the celebrations?'

'Yes, I do.'

'Isn't it unfair?'

'Yes, Sonny. It's very unfair.'

'And what are you planning to do about it?'

'I am going to burn the tent down,' he shouts.

Sonny slaps him. 'This is not how you are supposed to work. Your actions have to be subtle yet effective. Don't make promises that you'll not be able to fulfill. This is your first day with me and you are not doing well. It's better you stay quiet than make these blunders. Is that clear?'

'Yes, Sonny,' Akhil says.

'Good. Now just stay quiet and act only if you have a very good plan.'

As they cross House Number 12, Sonny looks up at a cluster of clouds, their edges shimmering in the sun. Sonny decides that, on reaching home, she is going to watch the weather forecast for Delhi. She hopes that heavy rainfall and thunderstorms will be predicted for the night, so that the tent poles collapse on the guests. She rarely watches the news. It doesn't make any difference to her life. Although, she had planned on inviting Ash over so that they could chat, and enjoy popcorn and Coke over the coverage of the Mumbai terrorist attacks that had taken place a week after their visit to Hotel Le M.

For the last couple of weeks, she had been secretly going to the guest room after Madaan had fallen asleep, and watching the news clippings. But she needed someone to share the immense emotion she felt – jealousy at the onlookers whose faces were being aired on national and international television, pleasure at all those trapped inside the hotel and battling for their lives.

Her strongest emotion was reserved for the ugly maid who had saved a four-year-old boy from N. House. Sonny was sure that she hadn't run up two storeys to rescue the boy who had been wailing next to the dead bodies of his parents. She must have requested one of the terrorists to spare her and the young boy in exchange for some cash and jewellery that she must have stolen from their cupboards or snatched from their dead bodies. After seeing the clipping of the ugly maid being hero-worshipped and being invited over to the young boy's home country, Sonny couldn't sleep for two nights. She couldn't believe that, despite being better looking, better educated and having more wealth, she had never appeared on television and had not gone outside India. She started hating Madaan for impregnating her just two months after their marriage and not giving her a chance to use her fertile mind to start a business. She also started hating her two sons who had never invited her over to Mumbai even once. Had she been there during the terrorist strike, she too could have rescued a young child and been on TV. That would have given her a free ticket to a foreign land and enhanced her social standing.

'Bastards!' she shouts.

'What happened?' Akhil asks nervously.

'Nothing. I was thinking. Anyway, did you miss out something I could see or comment on?'

'Not yet. This colony is rather quiet.'

'I know. But you're not performing well and may land both of us in trouble once we start going out.'

'Going out?' Akhil asks, puzzled.

'Yes. We'll start going to different places once you are trained.'

'What are we going to do?'

'You'll learn with time. I'm not going to pay you five thousand rupees just to accompany me on a one-hour walk.'

'Okay.'

The two have crossed the field with the old Post Office building and are standing outside House Number 16. Sonny sees a mountain of cement and bricks heaped before it. Gauri had already warned her that the owners of the house were planning to renovate it soon, but she had never taken the warning seriously. There were two reasons for her disbelief – Madaan had told her that the owners often delayed on even small bills for medicines and, she was too depressed about Ash and the Mumbai attacks to bother. Now, seeing the cement and bricks outside the house, Sonny feels a sense of urgency. Before she can even begin to act on it, Akhil runs towards the mountain and stomps on it. He picks up three bricks from the top of the pile and flings them on the pavement. They crumble the moment they hit the surface. Sonny feels relieved that Akhil is finally getting a hang of his job, although she would have preferred it if he had told her what he was about to do.

On their way ahead, Sonny tells Akhil that although she liked his attempt, it would have been better if they had just picked up one brick each and collected some cement and put it in their pockets. He had not achieved anything by scattering the cement or breaking the bricks as they could be used again. But, if he had applied his mind a little bit, then he would have stolen one brick and some cement. Over the course of twenty to thirty walks, that would have meant a visible loss for House Number 16. She warns him that he must be careful in the case of this house in particular, as it was very close to hers and she'd be able to see all the repair work and renovation from the balcony.

'Understood?' she asks.

'Yes Sonny,' Akhil says, controlling his laughter.

'Good.'

The two of them leave House Number 16 behind, although Sonny keeps looking back at the mountain of cement and bricks from time to time. Akhil makes use of this opportunity to stealthily slip out the folded paper from his trouser packet. He is pressing it against his thigh with his right palm and waiting for Sonny to turn around and focus on him. When she does, he quickly opens it and reads the instructions.

He can only read Instruction Number 4: Always ask about my dying mother-in-law. Always add 'dying' before 'mother-in-law' otherwise I'll get angry.

He folds the paper and puts it back in his trouser pocket just in time. Then he looks at Sonny and asks, 'So, how is your dying mother-in-law?'

Sonny gets excited, stops in her tracks and faces Akhil. He is looking nervous but she calms him down by gently taking his right hand and placing it between her slightly splayed legs.

'Don't you feel anything unusual?' she asks.

'Should I?'

'Of course, Akhil!'

'I just feel a bulge.'

Sonny lets go of his hand and the two start walking again.

'My mother-in-law has been suffering from a stomach infection for the past two weeks. Since we don't let any doctors see her for fear of being asked to admit her to a hospital, Madaan is assuming that it must have been caused by the tomato soup we were trying to feed her after she started rejecting the potatoes and porridge. Now, she shits four times a day and my whole day is spent holding a diaper in one hand, and a wet towel and room freshener in another. Yesterday, I told Madaan that I can't clean up after her anymore and that he should call his sister, Bela, over. Before he could respond, I added that if she loved her mother so much that she couldn't sleep, then she might as well come over and clean her shit. Madaan reminded me that his father had bequeathed the house to him on the condition that we should take care of his mother till her last breath.

Anyway, I called up Bela directly and told her that I was not well and would greatly appreciate it if she could come over and stay with her mother. She agreed, and the first thing I did after disconnecting was to hide the only packet of diapers behind a pile of clothes in my cupboard and wear the fresh one that was waiting to be tied around my mother-in-law. Now Bela will come home and see her beloved mother lying on the bed, drenched in her diarrhoea. I can always tell Madaan that the girl must have stolen the diapers. I'll probably have to scream at her, give her a slap or two, but at least I'll get what I want. I'll get my sister-in-law, whose husband is making millions and whose son is not losing his job despite the recession, to smell and clean her mother's shit like I have to.'

'Oh! That's strange.'

Sonny starts stomping on the pavement. 'You don't remember Instruction Number 1?' she screams.

'Yes, I do,' Akhil says.

'Then repeat it for me.'

'I know it Sonny,' he pleads.

'Repeat it, or I'll cut 1,000 rupees from your salary.'

'Okay. There is nothing strange about what the two of us do. We are suffering the most in this world. It is, then, only natural for us to feel bad when we see others happy, or insecure when we see others suffering more than us. But remember, the problem is not the two of us – it is the cruel world we live in.'

'Good. Now apply it in real life and never call anything we do 'strange'. It goes against our basic principle,' Sonny says sternly.

'Okay, Sonny.'

The two reach the small cement pedestal next to House Number 19. Two pots full of water are lying on top of it. Sonny looks around to see if anyone is watching her, then takes out a bottle of toilet cleaner. She passes it to a bewildered Akhil and motions him to pour it into the pots.

'Really?' he asks, baffled.

'Yes.'

'But that's not written in the instructions.'

'It is. Instruction Number 2. You will try your level best to make others suffer.'

'That's fine Sonny. But this can kill the person who drinks from it.'

'Person!' Sonny exclaims.

'Yes.'

'Or those cows because of whom I lost a major catch for my elder son, Gaurav?'

'I don't understand, Sonny,' Akhil says, looking lost.

'Just pour the toilet cleaner into the pots. No person drinks water from them. It is meant for the unruly cows that the milkman leaves to stroll on the pavements and graze in the field.'

'But what have the cows done to you?'

'Pour it and I'll tell you.'

Akhil goes up to the pedestal, opens the bottle of toilet cleaner and pours a small quantity into one of the pots. Sonny follows him, her steps more assured, her resolve more certain. She takes the bottle from him and empties it into the pots, then turns back to see Akhil staring at her, tears streaming down his eyes.

'Occupational hazard, Akhil!' Sonny exclaims and pats him on the back.

'Okay,' Akhil says in a muted tone.

On their way to the Kirby Place red light, Sonny tells Akhil that a few weeks ago, a rich man's only daughter had stumbled on Gaurav's pictures on a social networking site. She was instantly smitten by his looks, contacted him, and the two struck up a friendship. Just a week after they got in touch, the girl told her father about Gaurav. He was a bit hesitant after learning about their family background, but she refused to listen to him and even threatened to commit suicide if he didn't agree to the proposal. Her father agreed, but on one condition – he wanted to make sure that even if Gaurav's family wasn't well off, they should at least have some class and a decent standard of living. For that, he would have to visit their family home. Madaan got a call from the rich industrialist and a date was set for a meeting. Knowing that such an opportunity didn't come every day, Sonny made the girl clean the entire house for fifteen hours. She also had an argument with Madaan over whether they should keep his mother's door open or not, since she had developed a habit of wailing if left alone, despite the sleeping pills Sonny mixed in all her meals. Madaan wanted the rich man to know that one member of the family was ailing, but Sonny didn't. She told him that rich fathers were very possessive about their daughters and wouldn't like the prospect of their newly married daughter having to live under the same roof as a sick person. Madaan told her that he would tell the man in advance that their prospective daughter-in-law would not be expected to take care of the grandmother-in-law, but Sonny disagreed because this move on his part would give the girl an upper hand after the marriage and it would ruin Sonny's plans to extort money from the father. So, in the end, it was decided that Sonny's mother-in-law would be locked up with the maid, and a waiter would be hired to serve the industrialist. Sonny decided to entertain the man in her bedroom as the drawing room needed a new coat of paint. Since she didn't want him to be suspicious, she kept the door to the drawing room open, switched off all the lights and set up a mouse trap for everyone to see. She had decided to tell him that the maid had seen a big rat scurry inside.

The day the industrialist was to visit, Sonny and Madaan stood nervously on the balcony for hours to make sure that everything went right. Minutes before the industrialist was scheduled to arrive, two cows appeared at their gate, blocking the way. One of them started mooing while the other shat all over the pavement. Sonny started crying out for the milkman, but it was too late. The industrialist had already arrived in his BMW, and stepped right into fresh cow dung the moment he got out of his car. He immediately telephoned his daughter, screamed at her and left.

'We never heard about the girl from Gaurav again,' Sonny sighs.

'That's sad,' Akhil says.

'I know. I hope those cows come back to drink from the pots and die.'

'Okay,' Akhil says.

'What okay?' Sonny shouts.

'I mean, what can I say, Sonny? I just think you're a fucked up woman who is using me because I couldn't get a job after completing my MBA,' Akhil shouts.

'But your résumé says that you were willing to do anything to make money and that you loved the dark side of life,' Sonny argues.

'Yes, I had. But I never said that I was a psychopath or serial killer. You'll have to find someone else,' Akhil says indifferently.

'No. You won't leave me. You look just like Ash,' Sonny breaks down.

'Who is Ash?'

'He is my soul mate, but he's very sick.'

'Well, I hope you and your soul mate drink water from the pots instead of the innocent cows,' Akhil screams.

Sonny is about to hit him, when he pulls her by the hair and whacks her head against an electricity pole repeatedly. Sonny starts to struggle and cry for help, but Akhil's grip is rock solid. Suddenly, a crowd starts to gather. Akhil leaves Sonny and starts running. Sonny covers her bloody head with her hands. Bystanders offer her water or a lift, but she refuses all of them and starts walking towards Shastri Bazaar.

Sonny is sitting under the shade of an Asoka tree. in Sriganesh Garden. She had requested a couple who were leaving to give her a mask they were carrying – probably a disguise they used to make out and not be caught. She wore the mask, bought a cold drink and, feeling faint, decided to rest for a bit.

'Hi. I am Ash,' she hears a very familiar voice speaking to her.

She looks up to see Ash, also wearing a mask, holding his hand out to her.

'I am Sonny,' she says.

'I know.'

'What do you want, Ash?'

'The past. Us.'

'Are you sure?'

'Yes.'

The two are resting under the shade of the tree. Ash has taken off Sonny's mask and is gently daubing the blood on her forehead with a wet towel. A while later, he takes off his mask as well.

'I love you for you, Ash! I don't care about what I saw in the hotel's bathroom.'

'It was a mistake, Sonny.'

'I don't care, Ash. I just want you to be with me.'

'Then why didn't you take my calls?'

'I was too shocked, Ash. It took time for the scene to sink in.'

'And what about the letter?'

'What letter, Ash?'

He looks at her in surprise, then takes out a neatly folded piece of paper from his pocket.

'I made a copy in case you didn't get it,' he says.

She snatches the paper from him as if her life depended on it and, then, slowly slides down into his lap. She irons out the folds on it and starts reading.

'You write beautifully, Ash,' she says.

'What do you like?'

'The description of the hospital.'

'Okay. Go ahead.'

'B Positive friends! Ash, I didn't know you could be so funny,' Sonny laughs, rolling her head on his thighs.

'I can be Sonny, but only when I write.'

'What a bitch Pranita is! Vegetable for life... Time bomb waiting to explode!' Sonny says angrily. 'Let's add her to our list of victims, Ash. What do you say?'

'No, Sonny. Let her be.'

'Goldfish! Turtle! You have a peculiar taste in pets, Ash.'

'What's so peculiar about a goldfish and a turtle, Sonny?'

'They sound so exotic, Ash. As if only rich people can keep them.'

'Not at all.'

'Awww. You actually visited all those places to see if we had made an impact. Of course we did, Ash! Never doubt what the two of us do. Oh! And this is so funny. That Ellen from Le M recognised you and refused to talk about her short-lived trip.'

Sonny starts laughing out loud, rolling around in Ash's lap.

Once she finishes reading the letter, she folds the paper and moves her hand behind her back trying to feel Ash's pocket. Just then a tall, dark man appears before them. He starts dangling a few Polaroid pictures before Sonny and Ash. Sonny immediately gets up to take a closer look. She can see pictures of Ash and herself, while she was lying down, reading the letter. The pictures are very cleverly taken – Sonny brushing her wide open mouth against Ash's stomach while laughing at one of his phrases, or moving her hand to find his pocket, a gesture that made it seem like she was groping for his penis. Ash looks at the pictures and stands up, alarmed. The two of them exchange a look before Sonny asks, 'Who are you? What do you want?'

'I am the man who was made to masturbate to the picture of your dog, and whose girlfriend committed suicide after the two of us were found naked and shivering inside the bathroom.'

Before Sonny can say anything he adds, 'Madaan Chemists, 32 Mansarovar Garden. 23563245.'

'What do you want us to do?' Sonny asks.

'Yes. What do you want?' says Ash.

'Come to the bathroom.'

'For what?'

'Just come!'

Sonny and Ash are standing naked against the grimy wall inside the bathroom. The man is leaning against the wash basin. He has locked the door from inside. He takes out a pistol and brandishes it before them.

'She committed suicide. We didn't kill her,' Sonny shouts and starts crying.

'Yes, that's true,' Ash adds.

'I'm in no mood to listen to your defence. Which one of you wants to die first?'

The two of them look at one another before Sonny finally breaks the silence.

'Kill Ash,' she says. 'He is already suicidal and has no one to take care of. I have to look after my mother-in-law and two sons who are totally dependent on me.'

'What, Sonny?' Ash sobs.

'Ash should be third time lucky. He is of no use to anyone. At least I have some purpose.'

'So it will be Ash, first!'

'No!' Ash screams. 'Kill her. She beats her seven-year-old maid and lies to everybody. And she considers her mother-in-law and her sons great burdens.'

'I see,' the man says and points his gun at Sonny. Just as he pulls the trigger, she grabs hold of Ash and drags him before her. The bullet pierces Ash's chest. Sonny shoves the half-dead Ash towards the man like a shield and knocks him down, letting Ash fall on top of him. She grabs the man's pistol and strikes his head so hard that his skull cracks.

She puts on her clothes and opens the door.

She gives Ash's corpse a final look, turns around, and locks the door.

While walking past the entrance of Sriganesh Garden, she looks at the Polaroids of her and Ash.

'Bastard! You were a bastard Ash!' she shouts.

Chapter 3

Five Weeks Later.

Sonny is standing on her rooftop holding an air gun in her hand. She is looking down at the road, waiting for someone to pass by. A few cars and motorbikes have gone past but they moved too fast for her to take aim. She sighs and looks at her seven-year-old maid huddled in a corner of the terrace, rinsing clothes under the tap. Sonny had told her to turn it off while she scrubbed so that no water was wasted, but the maid seems to have forgotten. She is about to walk in her direction with her hand raised threateningly when she hears a noise from below.

She walks back to peer over the ledge, and sees two young medical interns, a boy and a girl, going back home from the army hospital. She bends down, squints, and takes aim. The yellow plastic pellet hits the girl on the head. She shrieks and drops her files and notebooks. The boy immediately kneels down and starts collecting her possessions, while the girl scratches her head and looks around. Sonny immediately turns back and sits down, out of sight, and starts laughing out loud. The maid looks at her and smiles. Sonny glares at her. She starts scrubbing the clothes even harder.

Minutes later, the doorbell rings. Sonny hopes that it is Bahadur, with the news that Jerry has finally been tracked down. She runs downstairs and opens the door.

Instead of Bahadur, she sees a woman smiling sadly at her. She is holding a black Labrador by the leash. The dog is panting and wagging his tail.

'Yes?'

'May I come in?'

'Who are you?'

'I am Rajni Ahuja. Ashwin Ahuja's mother.'

'Who is Ashwin Ahuja?'

'Oh! You probably know him as Ash.'

Suddenly, Sonny can't breathe. 'What do you want?' she manages to say.

'May I come in?'

'Alright.'

They are sitting on Sonny's bed. The dog has been unleashed and is curled up in a corner of the room, next to the TV.

'I am sorry about Ash,' Sonny says.

'I know. The fault is ours. We could never understand what was going on inside his head. Anyway, his father would never have approved of a homosexual relationship.'

'But what did the police say?'

'They're calling it a crime of passion.'

'How sad.'

'I know. I wish Ash had told me about his inclinations. I would have supported him. But the poor boy could never get rid of his depression.'

'He was taking medicines, wasn't he?'

'Yes. But nothing was working. I had taken him to all the top psychiatrists in town. All they did was change the medicine, or increase or reduce the dosage… I think there was something fundamentally wrong with my son.'

'I see.'

Rajni looks at the floor and starts crying.

'Would you like some tea?' Sonny asks awkwardly.

'No. I had come just to hand over Buzo to you.'

'You mean this dog?'

'Yes.'

'Why?

'I found a note in one of Ash's diaries. He had written that if anything happened to him, then Buzo should be handed over to his friend, Sonny. He had scribbled your address below that.'

'Really?' Sonny exclaims, unable to control herself.

'Yes.'

'You mean I can keep Buzo?'

'Yes.'

'And can I rename him Jerry?'

'Sure.'

'Jerry! Jerry!' Sonny shouts.

Buzo immediately runs to Sonny, wagging his tail. Sonny gets off the bed and starts petting him.

'Oh, Jerry! Thank you!'

'Anyway, I should go now,' Rajni says.

Sonny accompanies her to the door, bids her goodbye and runs back to her room shouting, 'Jerry! Jerry!'

Buzo runs towards her. She tries to lift him but the two of them fall back on the bed. Sonny rolls over the bed in pure joy.

Suddenly, a thought about Ash crosses her mind. She gets up from the bed, walks to the bedside and picks up a pair of scissors. She remembers the time she spent with her partner in crime. She knows she will never meet anyone as good as him. She runs the scissors over her wrist till it starts bleeding, then rushes to the bathroom.